Children of the Night | Tamar Paul-Cohen

To Elisha, my friend, my man, who allowed me to dream. Thank you for who you are and for who I am when I am with you.

To Gal, Arad, and Nadav---the most important creations in my life, you give it the real meaning.

Children of the Night
Tamar Paul-Cohen

Cover Design: Yifat Zezak Dromy
Cover image: shutterstock/hanapon1002's , Created by
Ilovehz - Freepik.com
Translated from the Hebrew: Susan Treister
Contact: tpaulcohen@yahoo.com

ISBN 9781729362891

T.C PAUL

CHILDREN OF THE Night

No one is free, even the birds are chained to the sky.
                                                          ~ **Bob Dylan**

The Law

Fate, many say, is not in our hands. Some go much further, and believe that fate is pre-determined and cannot be changed, but I was raised not to contend with my fate. All the people of the village of Xiyuan, in the Jiangxi district of Southern China, are born to the same fate, and end their lives sooner or later, in the same place. Many years passed before I understood that life in the village was governed by an almost impossible combination of our tradition and the law that decreed that each woman could get pregnant and give birth just once.

The few children were born in the one hospital in the area. Many women from the village would give birth at home, and the future of those children depended on the local chief of police.

The local chief was an ambitious man who would visit the villages every few days and look for the extra children who were born illegally. The law was quite clear: one child per couple. There were no exceptions and no dispensations. The chief and his corps would arrive in a village and search in the house of every single family. If they found an extra child, they took either the parents or the child. I have no idea what they did with them, but I never saw the children they took again.

The people in the village did not accept the evil decree,

and every couple in the village had more than one child. These children were called the "Children of the Night."

***

I was the first child born to my parents, and was considered a special case in the village. Besides the fact that I was a girl, and there were very few girls in the village, my mother told me that I had been born at a weight so low that the midwife gave her the feeling that chances were slim that I would survive, and suggested that maybe it would be better not to bond with me. But from the moment my mother saw my little face, she decided not to give up on me, that's what she told me. She wrapped her body around me, and didn't dare let go of me, even to bathe. My parents, Long and Guan-Yin Leyao, gave me the name Ming, meaning fate. Maybe they were thinking of their fate when they did not give up on me, and maybe in the name they gave me, they sought to give me hope that my fate would be different from theirs.

For two months my mother stayed at home in bed, and I was a completely integral part of her. Even when she got up to eat and drink, and she was indeed very careful about what she ate so as to be able to continue to feed me her milk, she did not disconnect my little body from her warm body. Every day I put on weight, and with each passing day, my body covered more and more of her gaunt figure.

Every evening my father returned from work in the field and asked to hold his daughter in his arms, which would break the physical connection between my mother and myself and allow her to rest a bit; and every evening my mother would smile and say, "Maybe tomorrow she'll be big enough."

I remember her warm body, the smell that clung to her, of laundry and sweat. I felt how she sometimes tried to do housework while I was nursing at her warm breast. My mother's touch was the best welcome there could be into our world.

The days passed. When my father saw that my mother's movements had slowed down, he understood that I had grown. One evening, he returned home and found my mother stirring a pot of rice on the stove, singing a children's song. His eyes looked for the little baby that had just let go of her mother's body, and found me lying alert in their bed. For the first time in his life, he picked me up in his arms, and his eyes filled with tears. "She looks so much like you," he said to my mother.

For my first six years, my mother was home. In our village, there were no social classes, everyone was lower class, and everyone worked in the fields, both women and men. Few were privileged like my mother to work in the packing house, though she stopped working when I was born.

My father would go out to work early in the morning in the village rice field, so I had my mother all to myself. At home she would sing to me, and in the morning she would walk with me outside on the unpaved paths of the village, letting me soak up the warm rays of the sun, which kept my cheeks rosy throughout my childhood. My mother would invite friends to our house who were also at home with young babies. I remember my first friends very clearly. I loved their visits. We were left on the floor to play together. I remember how we looked each other over while our mothers sipped tea and chatted. My mother would put a collection of objects in front of us, and ask that we create something together. The towers always fell on us, but we didn't give up. We tried again and again, knocking them down each time, and we always had a good laugh – from the crash of the falling objects, from the little things that we had. We always had a good time.

We would eat together what the mothers had prepared, and fell asleep all together in my parents' bed. When they returned to their homes, I was glad to be left alone with my mother. I loved to lean on her bony shoulder, and smell in her hair the odors of the house, and the aroma of her cooking, and hear her sing into my ear, whispering words that I didn't always understand, while her body swayed in a slow dance.

Our village, like many other villages in the area, was very picturesque: sharp mountains wrapped in vegetation on the horizon, their tips exposed, looking smooth and tall. I spent time every day looking at the mountains, which were mesmerizing. The vegetation changed color every season: in the summer, the slopes of the mountains turned yellow, and the stones that protruded were surprisingly dark; in autumn the colors turned red, and the mountains seemed covered in blood. In the winter, the peaks were white, water flowed from the mountains to the streams, and the smell of clean snow was everywhere.

The summer was long. I always waited for winter throughout the hot and sticky summer; and during the frozen winter that forced us to stay inside, I wished that summer would come so I could go out and play. And then winter would return once again, bringing with it the cold wind that blew through the mountains and brought the smell of snow down to the village.

The village was built along a flowing stream that received its water from the melting snow, which provided most of the running water to the village. There were more than fifty houses in the village. Under some of them tunnels had been dug, whose walls were sealed with mud. These tunnels were the hiding place of the children of the night.

***

While the sun shone outside, the children of the night spent their days in the darkness that was inside. Sometimes, the mothers wanted their children to get some sun, and would take them to their work in the fields, and hide them among the piles of gathered grain. The children would fall asleep with one side of their faces exposed to the sun, and based on this one cheek, the darker one, it was possible to identify most of them.

My mother was happy with the one daughter born to her, and never wished for other boys or girls. But there were nights when I would pretend to be asleep, and I heard my father try to convince her to have another child. My mother would say "no" every time, and the conversation ended.

I, unlike my father, did not wish for a brother, since I was growing up with boys who were like brothers to me. But in the mornings that came after the nightly persuasion attempts, I would ask my mother if she could bring me a sister, because I had not yet met any girls, and she would smile at me, and continue with her work.

My mother, who hadn't returned to work and was home with me, offered to look after the neighbors' children in our house, in exchange for some of their parents' daily wages. Thus I grew up in a tiny house with another three babies my age. The three boys were all called Chang, the most common name in our village, and in China in general. Chang 1 was the thinnest, and his skin was very dark. He was the mischievous one in the group, and also the crybaby. Chang 2 was a quiet dreamer, and we always had to wait until he woke up from his afternoon nap. He moved slowly, and even though we did not play with him much, he always smiled, and never cried. Chang 3 was chubby, even though he ate the least. Many times I heard my mother get angry with him, when he tried to pull at things in the house and knock them down. He always wanted to know what was hiding on the other side of everything; I liked to peek, too.

***

Our house in the village was no different from any other. The entrance door was made of wooden beams, and it looked like that of every other house in the village; only the inside of the house distinguished one family from another. Since most of the families remained small, with few children, the people could live in the little houses their entire life.

Our house was especially colorful because my mother loved color. She lay fabrics of different colors on the furniture, or tied them on the windows, creating an interesting and non-uniform texture. My mother always thought that colors affect our mood, and that this added happiness to life. I, who was born into all this colorfulness, did not know that peace could be found in a single color. When I grew up and was forced to clean single-colored, white rooms, I remembered the colorfulness of my parents' house, and along with the tears always brimming in my eyes, a smile came over my lips.

Our door was exactly in the middle of the house. On the right side of the door, near the wall, stood a table that my mother used for preparing food. On the adjacent wall was a fireplace surrounded by piles of wood blocks ready for burning. The fireplace was used to warm the house in the winter, but it was mainly used for cooking. My mother would prepare rice for us every day, and added some vegetables to the dish. Every few days my father would come home with chunks of chicken, and the next day my mother would prepare the chicken for us to eat.

On the other side of the door hung a pink curtain, behind which was my parents' bed. At the foot of the bed stood a cradle that had been passed down from generation to generation in the village, and when I grew up, they put out another bed for me.

Right in front of the entrance door, my mother laid out a mat covered with a mix of all the colors of the rainbow, and even a few other shades, and that was the center of my life. On this mat I crawled, played, grew, and learned to love life in my village. This mat was also used by Chang 1, Chang 2, and Chang 3, and together we would eat, play, listen to songs that my mother sang to us, and sleep in the afternoon, in the area between the tiny kitchen and the beds.

When the sun set, the parents of the Changs would come to pick them up. I knew that when they left, my father would come home. After my mother helped him take off his clothes, and bathed him in the tub in the yard, my father would lie down with me on the mat, and bounce me up in the air. My mother in the background would call him in for supper, but he would always first perform this ritual with me, and only after that would he sit down to eat. I was content. My development was much faster than that of the three boys. At eight months, I was already crawling all over the house, while they just cried in frustration watching me get to every corner. At 10 months, I already walked from wall to wall, and I already had pronounced my first words: "hot" and "come." "Hot" because my mother always warned me not to go near the burning fireplace, and "come" I learned from her encouraging the boys to move forward.

***

One evening, my father returned from work and found me playing with Chang 2 at my mother's feet; she was just about to wash our dishes. My father threw me in the air, and his sweaty, dirt-streaked face broke into a smile. His face was angular, but his smile pulled it in a funny way. His eyes almost closed whenever he smiled. When my mother asked him to first wash his hands and face, he put me down on the ground, but immediately picked up Chang 2, with the look on his face of someone who had waited all day to smile at a baby. Only when my father had put down Chang did he ask my mother, "They didn't come to take him?" My mother wiped her hands on the yellow apron tied around her waist, and helped my father take off his shirt. "They're apparently still at work," she said. "He'll eat with us, and we'll wait for them together."

Chang's parents had not arrived even after a very long time, and my father went out to look for them. My mother bathed us and put us in white pajamas, and in her sweet voice hummed notes that always relaxed my body, and helped me sink into a deep sleep. But Chang's presence was strange to me, and I didn't manage to fall asleep. I heard my father come back, and despite his attempts to speak quietly, I understood that something had happened to Chang's father.

The next day, there was a funeral in the village. We stayed home with my mother, and continued our daily routine: we played, crawled, laughed, and cried. And the tears were not necessarily for the loss of parents, just the crying of a baby who needs something.

After she had lost her main source of livelihood, Chang's mother understood that she could not leave him with us anymore. But my mother, who had gotten used to the four children in her house, asked Chang's mother to pay only for the food that she made him, and to everyone's delight, Chang 2 remained at our house.

The four of us already knew how to walk, and it was hard for my mother to supervise us when we went out on nice days. When my father noticed this, he decided to build us a small wagon that my mother could use to push us around the village. After he returned from work, he collected wood and asked one of the neighbors to help him put together a wagon that looked a little like a chariot. Dewei-Hu, who lived next door, immediately agreed to help my father. Dewei-Hu did not have any children yet, and was happy to spend his free time on this task. The wagon needed to be built of a relatively small amount of wood, so that my mother would be able to push it easily. It needed to be strong, and have enough room for four little children to sit in it. There were two wooden beams at the base of the wagon, and in time, we learned not to let our feet slip between them. The upper frame was made of four beams, and at the sides were additional beams, unevenly spaced. Dewei-Hu obtained a pair of wooden wheels from a broken plough, and mounted them in the center of the wagon. My mother padded four wooden squares that we used as seats, and sewed to each seat a fabric pocket with openings for our legs, which my father attached to the wood with small nails. Each pocket was a different color--I always sat in the seat with the red pocket, Chang 1 in the yellow, Chang 2 in the green, and Chang 3 in the seat with the orange pocket. Thanks to the fabric pockets into which we stuck our legs, we sat firmly in our seats, and the wagon remained balanced.

This was how we walked around the village, waving to everyone we passed. The village children looked at us with great envy; they too wanted a wagon, and they too longed for friends. The streets of the village were delineated with pebbles; the street was meant for cars that rarely appeared in the village, and we would walk on either side of the street. Our wagon was so big, that my mother drove us along the marked road. Though the way was very bumpy, the ride was always an experience that we would not give up. When we rode around, we always felt that we were traveling very far, even if the trip was very short. The wagon raised us up, and the feeling that we were traveling around the village like little emperors caused us great delight. Most of the trip we laughed, mostly from the sensation caused by the jerky road, but maybe also from embarrassment. We were the royalty of the village at least an hour a day.

Dewei-Hu began to work nights building wagons for the people in the village. Wagons for small children with one or two seats became a common sight in our village, and my mother sewed seats with safety pockets to hold the children so they would not move or fall from their places. Word of the practical children's wagons spread to the neighboring villages, and in a short time, Dewei-Hu had left his job in the field, and devoted all his time to building the wagons. Through his customers, we started to hear stories about life behind the snowy mountains.

***

When I turned six, I could go out and play by myself, and my mother returned to her job in the packing house, in the vegetable-sorting warehouse. For many hours I hung around with my friends in the fields. Our playground was on the north side of the village. It actually had two rides that had been broken for many years, but we still managed to play on them, improvising various games. There was a merry-go-round that had fallen off its axle and was resting on the ground, but it was unstable and wobbled from side to side. We would sit in it and rock it forcefully. Whenever someone felt he could no longer stand the shaking, he would get off, and we played like this until there was one person left, and he was the winner. I was always one of the first to get off as I was prone to nausea. The other piece of equipment consisted of metal bars that had held two swings which had disappeared long before I was born. We put rocks under the bars, and stood on them so we could reach the upper bar, which we hung from. The one who fell last was the winner. I loved this piece of equipment, and many times I managed to stay up the longest. The boys always said it was thanks to my small body and low weight, and I answered that I was just stronger. On rainy days, I invited my friends to my house, and at home we would play games with small rocks that we would gather, or fantasy games we invented. I was content.

One evening, after my parents came back from work and we sat down to eat supper, I asked them, "Why are there no other girls in the village? Why are there only boys my age?", and for the first time, my mother explained that the government, represented by the police officers that sometimes came to the village, had prohibited its citizens from bringing more than one child into the world. My mother tried to explain why this was so, but I didn't understand, or maybe I didn't want to understand; I just wanted to play with other girls. I knew of only one other girl in the village who had a twin brother, but she played only with him.

One night, when I was seven, I was late coming home. That night was the first time I encountered the children of the night. That night, my fate was sealed.

***

That afternoon, it seemed that I had managed to take myself far away from my house. I left the area of the houses, and walked into the open fields. The workers that went up and down from the fields popped up in the colorful landscape that stretched to the mountains, and from a distance it looked like they were playing a piano spread over the horizon. I could see that there were still many of them at work, and I was distracted by my wanting to count how many workers there were in each row. The sun had already set, and I had not taken into account the time it would take me to return to the village, as I had promised my parents. I picked up my pace; I didn't want to anger or worry my mother. Night had already fallen by the time I reached the paths of the village, but I was not afraid to walk on trails that were so well-known to me.

All of a sudden, at a curve in the path, I noticed a large band of children. They were all of different ages, boys and girls, older than me and younger than me. They didn't look any different, on the contrary, they looked exactly like the boys I already knew, and they were running excitedly down the street. Something in their uniform look made me curious. Suddenly, I longed to join them. Maybe they have other games? I wondered. Maybe they do other things that I would like to do. My head was full of questions, and I watched them, fascinated. For the first time, I saw many girls my age, and I wanted to ask them to stop for a moment and talk to me.

I stood at the side of the road, frozen in my place. The children didn't stop playing when they saw me. They ran around me, boys and girls together, laughing and playing wildly, and only after a long time did I manage to continue on my way home.

Our children of the night seemed free to me. I wanted to be free like them.

***

From the day I came across the children of the night, all I wanted was to join in their games. My mother was vehemently opposed to my joining them. All my attempts to convince my father to let me go out at night were in vain---until the day my mother received word of a relative who was ill, and she was forced to travel for a few days to another village. My father arranged for one of the produce delivery trucks to take my mother, and I was left alone with my father.

One night, I waited with closed eyes for my father to fall asleep. My heart pounded, but my curiosity was stronger. I left the house quietly, and walked toward the path where I had first seen the children of the night. I stood in the place where they had scampered around me, and I imagined that I heard their cheerful cries. The wind whistled, the leaves rustled, but the children of the night were nowhere to be found. Then suddenly I saw them. They shone in the darkness. Two girls around my age, whose faces glowed in a round smile, called me to play jump rope with them. I ran toward them and jumped high, higher than the mountains. I felt so happy. I did this every night, and every night, I was free. Free and happy.

When my mother returned, I told her right away what I had been doing. It made her sad, but she understood, maybe for the first time, that she would not be able to continue to prevent me from going out at night. And thus, like the children of the night, I turned the night into day. The children of the night slept during the day in their basements, and I also slept in my house. And when darkness came, when it was clear that the chief of police would not be coming, I went outside to play with them. The children of the night were accustomed to not talking during the day, and I quickly learned to do the same. During the day, I spoke only with my parents, before I went to sleep, and at night I spoke and played with my new girlfriends, and I felt free and light.

Seyoung was my best friend. She was the funniest girl in the village, round like her mother. She always told funny stories, and was always falling or tripping, and laughed at her own unsteadiness. Every evening when I left my house, I walk to her house, where she was waiting for me, so that we could walk together to the center of the village.

Very quickly, the three Changs also joined the children of the night, and though they were like brothers to me, I gradually stopped playing with them, and found myself in a group of girls who became my best friends. As time went on, the Changs also found new friends---at first I was angry when I saw them playing and they didn't invite me to join, then I would walk by them ostentatiously, calling their name and waving to them, so that everyone would see, and know that we were friends, and finally I became busy with my own new friends, and just glanced in their direction from time to time, to see what they were doing.

Time passed, and my schedule was always the same. I woke up in the afternoon, and started to prepare for supper with my parents. I waited for them to return from work, and add the vegetables or the meat to the water that I had already boiled for soup. And at night, I would wander to the usual place, and play with the children of the night, and I felt free and happy.

After the Silence

That night, when there was no sign forewarning what was about to happen to the entire village, it was relatively cool for the season, but we went outside to play anyway. A noise we had never heard before was approaching the village. As the sound intensified, we discerned a convoy of black cars that stopped on the main street.

Cars were not unheard of in the village. Occasionally, cars came to the village, most often that of the chief of police, but this time there were many cars. At first, they looked like a swarm of large black ants, then like large and threatening war machines. The noise the cars made when they traveled on the limestone road was heard throughout the village, and the dust raised by the wheels scattered ashy granules in the air. Everyone who heard the approaching convoy froze in place. The sound of the children of the night playing and laughing around the village was replaced by the noise of gravel crushed by the whirling tires, and the dense air that spread throughout the village immediately silenced the joyful voices of the children.

At that time, I was walking with my friend Seyoung to meet another two girls, to make our usual tour of the village. We stopped in front of the approaching convoy, and the noise grew, as the cars advanced toward us. Seyoung grabbed my hand and pulled me to the edge of the path. Slowly the procession of black cars emerged, and following them were higher vehicles, giant trucks designed for transporting crops. When the vehicles passed us, the dust clogged my throat and stung my eyes, which were fixed to the scene.

For a brief moment, when all the cars stopped, there was silence. And I would yearn for this silence and everything that had come before it, because after it came the devastation.

***

The policemen got out of the black cars. Soldiers in uniform jumped from the open trucks and started to run toward the children who stood along the paths. Screams of terrified children mixed with shrieks of parents trying to prevent the soldiers from pushing the children up onto the trucks, as if loading rebelliousbeasts.

Seyoung was taken by a soldier a moment before they took me, a short moment that left a long memory of sharp pain that pierced my chest and shook my entire body. The pain was replaced by an immobilizing fear when the soldier reached me, grabbed me by the arm, and pulled me to the truck. I tried to restrain our progress by digging my feet into the hard earth, but the soldier was strong and I was fragile, and felt that I did not have the strength or ability to resist. The soldier picked me up and threw me into the truck, and I hit the railing around the enclosure. The trucks had become temporary prisons for the children whose fate had suddenly turned upside down on them, and their lives were about to change forever.

Despite the pain in my foot, I stood up, and was thus able

to see the commotion taking place in the village. I saw soldiers dragging children, and parents trying to grab the clothes of the soldiers and prevent them from taking the children. I looked for my parents, but at that stage I did not manage to identify any faces in the tumult. The darkness and the dust still floating in the air created the appearance of figures and shadows with no clear features. The sounds mingled together and merged with the sights.

The truck I had been thrown onto began to fill up. Two soldiers that stayed on it stretched out their arms to lift up the children that the soldiers swung from below. I saw Jiali raised forcefully up to the truck. Her head hit the railing, and she started to shriek that her head was broken. The policeman did not miss a beat. He didn't even look at the girl that he threw in, or at what had happened to her; he just pushed her into the corner, clearing space to load on more children. I tried to find Jiali, was her head really broken? I was in the far corner from her, and the many other children who had been loaded onto the truck hid her from me. I tried to make my way to her, while I looked for my parents in the foggy landscape of the villagers fighting the policemen from all sides. I also felt the blow to my head. Later I felt it in every part of my body; everything hurt me, and I wanted to throw myself back out.

Instead of crying, shouts of pain came out of my throat, sharp pain, shouts that turned into screams that carried the remains of my voice. The other children didn't move. Everyone cried and looked for their parents through the barrier. For a second I saw Jiali—she got up and held onto someone beside her. Her head did not look like it was bleeding, and I was comforted by the view of her head in one piece. I stopped screaming.

Many parents that I knew congregated around the trucks in an attempt to release their children. I continued to look for my parents; I didn't understand yet why we had been thrown onto the trucks. I could only sense that something bad was happening.

From the side of the truck, I stood and held onto the barrier so as not to fall from the load of children pushing around me; I saw Liang's parents struggling with a policeman; they were holding their son's legs and trying to pull him toward them. The sights managed to settle the confusion and arouse my fear. I joined all the children on the truck, and began to cry. I looked for my parents, I wanted them to pull me out too, I wanted to get off the truck.

The commotion was quieted by the sounds of gunfire. A baby's cries broke the silence, and then the voice of the police chief echoed through the village: "If you continue to disturb the soldiers in their work, I will use weapons." He stopped talking and then commanded his soldiers: "Let's go, continue!"

The children were now being loaded faster. The dust had started to settle, and I continued to look all around for my parents. All of a sudden, I saw the figure of my mother running toward me. She recognized me on the truck; she got close to it and screamed to the soldier standing next to me: "My daughter Ming is not one of the children of the night; she's an only child." But the soldier didn't look at her; he didn't even move. My mother screamed at me, "Ming, don't be afraid, I'll make sure they take you off," and she ran to the chief of police, waving a piece of paper.

I had never seen her like that. She charged at the chief like a beast of prey; and when she stood in front of him, one of the police officers stopped her. "My daughter is my first-born and only child; you can't take her!" she shouted at him and waved the document from the hospital. The police chief remained tense, even though my mother was very close to him. He motioned with his hand to a police officer standing next to him, and ordered her removed from him with the wave of his hand.

The chief did not move from his place and continued to observe the children being put on the trucks. But my mother, who would not give me up, not when I was born, and not on the day when a truck took me away, struggled with the policeman, and then with another policeman who grabbed her too. Again and again she screamed at the police chief that I was her only daughter, and that I was not a child of the night.

I was all choked up. Air wouldn't go into my lungs. The screams I wanted to let out could not be heard. Everything inside was ripped to shreds. The railing that I was leaning on felt like it was sizzling and burning my hand. There were policemen all around who kept me from running to my mother. She was being held by two other police officers, and she continued to shout and move wildly in their hands until she finally fainted and fell to the ground.

I also fell into a bottomless abyss. I continued to fall, burning, breaking up into small parts, praying to wake up from the nightmare in broad daylight. The pain was terrible, my whole little body hurt, my legs could no longer carry me, and my heavy head fell and I didn't have the strength to pick it up. The fierce pain flowed through my blood and into every corner of my body. Every heartbeat hurt, ever breath burned. That's how I remembered my mother for the entire period that I was with the children of the night in the Artung children's home on the southern border of China. The picture of my mother screaming, struggling with the policemen to protect me and fainting kept me going during all the difficult and sad moments. I didn't want to disappoint her that she had chosen to bring just one daughter into the world, and during all the years I knew that I had to hold out and try to return to the village.

***

The fear and the cold bound us together on the truck. We all crowded into the center, and the soldiers started to come up too, until we were pushed to the end closest to the driver's seat. The trucks moved together, and it was still possible to hear the shrieks of the children and the parents who tried to approach us and were pushed back by the soldiers using the butts of their rifle.

The large vehicles moved slowly, circling the village and leaving it on the entrance road. The sounds from the village became distant, and the screams of the children on the trucks turned into crying that became fainter and fainter as the trucks drove on. The darkness prevented us from seeing anything, but the trip on unpaved roads was long and bumpy. I felt the bile rising in my throat, and I opened my mouth to let cold air in. It was a desperate attempt to prevent what happened anyway a few minutes later. I vomited the entire contents of my stomach. Unfortunately, the truck was so crowded that I couldn't move to the railing of the truck, and I sprayed uncontrollably what I had been eating lately on everyone who stood around me, and then I started to cry.

I couldn't say clearly what exactly hurt me more: the cold in my face, the emptied stomach, the chest whose muscles all cried with me, or my heart that was alone on the truck racing into the dark. I felt that this ride would never end. The uncertainty still didn't disturb me, because I was too preoccupied with the pains enveloping me. For a while I heard nothing, I sat frozen and suffered in silence. I hadn't noticed how much time had passed, but loud crying woke me from my stillness. I looked around for the person crying, and not far from me, I saw Chang 1's little brother Deshi.

I pushed away the two girls who were blocking my way to him, and pulled him to me. I hugged him tightly, and leaned his head under my chin in an attempt to quiet him. "Deshi, I promise you that I'll take care of you, calm down, you are with me now," I whispered in his ear without understanding the significance of my words at that time.

***

There is no doubt that my new role caused me to forget about the pains and the thoughts of the destruction. I was soon concentrating on the things I had to say to Deshi. "You are like my little brother, like your brother Chang was," I declared quietly in his ear, "I'll stay with you as if we're from the same family." In my heart, I hoped I would be able to keep the promises that came out of my mouth like what I had spewed previously on everyone who was standing near me. Deshi's crying gradually weakened, and I was glad that he had not let go of me.

I looked at the darkness that was around me, and tried to identify the figures surrounding me. I noticed that one of the girls I had pushed away was Anchi. I looked at her and remembered that her big brother came to play with us sometimes, while her mother and my mother sat and chatted. I also remembered that he had stopped coming and I hadn't understood why. When I met Anchi wandering around at night, I figured that her mother had been forced to stay at home, and could no longer come to us.

Anchi was younger than me, and so we hadn't spoken much at the gatherings in the village, besides a few pleasantries and quick smiles. She was very pretty, her symmetrical face was round, but not overly so, and her lips were always too red. Now I turned to her: "Anchi, come hold on to me too." Anchi hesitated, maybe she was embarrassed. I moved toward her, and pulled Deshi with me. "Come Anchi, we are family, come hold on to us too. "The gentle girl put her hand on Deshi's back, and looked down. The truck continued its bumpy ride, and we tried to hold out together.

Suddenly, the trucks stopped, and the police chief got out of his car, and came to talk with the soldiers' commanders. After a few minutes, the police officers' cars turned right, and the trucks continued to move in a convoy. Many children were already sleeping on the floor of the truck, and I was still hugging Deshi tightly. "Should we lie down on the floor?" I whispered in his ear, and without waiting for his answer, I pulled him and Anchi down and tried to find us space. Deshi immediately fell asleep in my arms. For the first in my life, and I was only 12, I understood that Deshi's fate was also in my hands. I didn't manage to cry.

I woke up in a panic to a loud squeal. This was the second truck that apparently had had trouble stopping, and the squealing of the brakes woke up all the children and soldiers who had fallen asleep. The morning had arrived to greet us, but none of us smiled back. Most of the children who woke up started crying and screaming at the sight of the trucks stopping at an unknown place.

With so much desperate crying all around, I also could shriek without anyone noticing. Those who did not cry just stared at what was going on in shock and fear. The pain flooded my body again, and the fear that something bad would happen to all of us crammed horrific thoughts into my head.

Deshi clung to me and hugged me even harder, but didn't cry. I was busy trying to return the circulation to my numb legs, and had released my hold on Deshi. He responded with awful crying. No hug would help calm him down. "Deshi, please shhhh. I am here with you. I am taking care of you!" I shouted. He continued to scream. I hugged him again, and he still wouldn't stop crying.

The crying of the children grew stronger as the sun came up, and it was possible to see. I looked at the two trucks parked nearby and tried to find Seyoung. I remembered the moment that she too was taken---her cheeks, which were always too red, suddenly seemed pale and expressionless. Her narrow eyes had never seemed so open. I remembered that she had been taken before me, and I knew that she wasn't on my truck. I did not find her in the other trucks either. For years later, everywhere I would be, I would always find myself looking for her.

***

Long minutes passed, and Deshi's crying stopped only when one of the soldiers decided to put an end to it. He looked at us as if we were one entity, and roared, "Quiet at once!" Deshi became silent, and his gaunt body shook in my hands. I wrapped my arms around him and tried to stop the shaking.

Another friend from the village joined us, joining in the hug, and she whispered in his ear, "It's okay, we are together." In the meantime, there was more squealing, and the back door of the truck opened to allow us to get off the truck. In contrast to what had happened in the village, where we were thrown into the trucks, now they let us get off slowly and carefully so we wouldn't get hurt. In front of us, there was a long one-story building surrounded by unplowed fields that looked nothing like the landscape of our village.

We walked in one big bunch to the building on which was hung a large sign with Chinese writing that I could not read. I remembered how my mother would put me to bed and say, "One day, you'll leave the village and travel, to learn how to read and write, and when you come back, you'll read stories to me." Those were her words every evening after she would tell me her stories, which she had heard from others, or made up herself just to tell me at bedtime.

Deshi reached his hand out to me and we went into the large hall at the entrance to the building. There, for the first time since we were separated, I saw Seyoung from afar, and I smiled for the first time. We were asked to stand along the walls. The room was huge, and only one window on the opposite wall let the sun's rays in. The color gray was prominent. The walls were bare, and it seemed that they had been painted very quickly, without waiting for them to dry before spreading on the next coat. The only picture on the wall was a large picture of Mao, hanging on the wall across from us. I knew that picture from the gathering house in the village. There, too, hung a large picture of Mao on the wall. I remember that my father had told me that Mao was a popular leader who had started the revolution. But since I hadn't been interested,

I didn't remember which revolution.

The floor was cement mixed with rocks and pebbles. There was no furniture in the room, only a long wooden pole with nails affixed, a kind of rack that I'd seen once at a friend's house in the village, but this pole was very long, and it was possible to hang the coats of all the people in our village on it. There was only a single brown hat on the rack, as if someone had forgotten to take it when he left.

We stood very close together. The soldiers remained at the entrance and counted the children who went in. We waited in silence for something to happen. I was sure that everyone wanted to wake up from the nightmare, but we couldn't even guess what exactly had happened, because everything had happened far from the village, and even further from the thoughts of children.

All of a sudden a round figure with short black hair came in, and one of the soldiers stood in the center of the room and announced, "This is the honorable Ms. Ushi-He! Ms. Ushi-He is the principal of the children's home here, and from now on, she will be telling you what to do and when." His voice, which quieted somewhat after the loud announcement, still echoed in the entire room. "I suggest that you behave very well, and be very polite, because from here you'll be sent directly to prison, and you'll never see your village again." He finished his words in a scream, turned to the door, and pointed to the round figure saying, "Okay, Ms. Ushi-He, they're all yours." He left the room and all the soldiers walked stiffly out of the room.

Ms. Ushi-He stepped to the center of the room and began speaking. Her voice was not very pleasant, but the noise of the engines was louder than it, and she stopped talking and waited with her hands stiffly behind her back until there was silence again. Her hair was short, and she wore men's clothes; from afar, she looked like a short, chubby man, and as she approached, her angry figure became clearer.

"If you behave like good children and don't make problems, you'll be able to grow up in comfortable quarters," she said, "but if you are disruptive or impolite, you'll be sent to horrible places." There were again sounds of weeping in the room, and in response, Ms. Ushi- He raised her voice, which was already loud and yelled, "The tears will not help anyone here. Stop it at once!" Though it took a while for the weeping to stop, silence returned to the room and we were asked to sit on the cold floor until the staff came in to register us.

The Registration Lady

The principal left the room and returned with a woman who looked older and taller than her. Her hair was very long and pulled back, and she held in her hand a stool and an object that I couldn't identify. The tall woman sat next to Ms. Ushi-He and put the black object, which I later identified as a binder, on her lap. "Now come up to me one by one and we'll register you. Tell me your name and age."

The frightened children stood in line before the registration lady, and I was among them. For a moment, I thought that I could be anyone else, so that when I ran away, they wouldn't know who I really was. I thought I would lie about my name and age, because there were so many children there, how would they know that I had lied? My legs suddenly trembled just from the thought of it; I understood that I had to focus all the time on any possibility to return to the village. I thought about this all the way to the registration lady, and one thought was especially terrifying: I understood that if my mother would indeed be looking for me, I would have to be identified by my real name. I felt that I was brave in that I was expecting my mother to come and get me. I wanted to believe that all I had to do was be patient and do whatever I was told until my parents came and explained the mistake that was made in my regard. This pleasant thought was cut short when Deshi came and hugged me from behind. My legs trembled again, and I turned around to him, returned the supportive hug, and held on to him, also so I wouldn't fall. I felt weak, I tried very hard to continue standing and hugging him, and I hoped that both of us would manage not to stumble.

The whole way to the registration lady, I could think only of my mother who was coming to take me home. Afterward, other thoughts came through about Deshi: How would I leave little Deshi alone in this place? How could I convince everyone that I had promised to always take care of him? How would I explain to my mother when she came to take me home that I must take Deshi with me? He was, after all, Chang's little brother who is actually my little brother. How would I explain to Ms. Ushi-He that he must return to the village with us, and that I wouldn't let him stay at that place, far from his parents and from me? I would have to explain that my soul had become tied to his soul at the fateful moment when we were cut off from the village, and that now I wanted to take him with me. These thoughts brought tears to my eyes, my legs did not stop trembling, and only Ms. Ushi-He's screams for "quiet at once!" returned me to that cold, gray room that I would be in for many more days.

It was finally my turn to go up to go up to the registration lady. When I approached, I saw her pleasant face. Maybe she even smiled at me. I told her my whole name and my age, 12, and I said that I was a firstborn, and that my mother would be coming to take me home soon. "There was a misunderstanding," I said heatedly. "I was walking around at night with a girlfriend, but I am not one of the children of the night, I am a firstborn and only child."

The registration lady looked up from the page and her eyes climbed up my body until they met mine. "Yeah, of course," she said sarcastically. "You and all the dozens of children here, you're all firstborn. You're all only children. None of you are children of the night, by chance you were playing outside in the middle of the night." And she broke out into forced laughter.

***

When I woke up on the mattress in the room that was spread full of mattresses, I remembered only the smile of the registration lady.

"She woke up," I heard Seyoung yell, and all the children ran to me.

"What happened?" I asked Seyoung as she hugged me as if we hadn't seen each other for weeks.

"You fainted in front of the registration lady. Something caused her to laugh really loudly, and you fainted and fell. The principal asked us to help take you to the room, and you've been sleeping for a long time." Seyoung breathed heavily from worry, but gradually calmed down.

"You really had me worried. I thought that I was going to lose you. Don't you dare faint again; you hear me? It's hard enough for me, and the way this place looks, I have a feeling it's going to get even harder."

"What does that mean, it's going to get even harder?" I asked Seyoung, hoping to hear that she was exaggerating.

"It's the strangest place I've ever seen in my life." Seyoung smiled sadly. "I've actually not seen many places in my life, but this is a very strange place, the rooms are sad and empty, and there is nothing here, just two strange women with frightening voices and looks that can make us faint, like what happened to you.

"When you fainted, Ms. Ushi-He came up to you, and after she understood that you had tried to convince the registration lady that you're a first born, she also laughed at you, and both women left you on the floor, they just pointed at two children and motioned that they should take you out of there." Seyoung was speaking so fast, that sometimes I found it difficult to follow what she was saying. "They didn't even care that you'd fallen, they just laughed at you and what you said."

Seyoung continued, "Ms. Ushi-He explained that every day we will gather in the large hall. Besides that, there are two rooms with mattresses for us to sleep on. There is also a hallway with other rooms, but we can't go in there. Ms. Ushi-He stressed that we are strictly prohibited from going there. There is a water faucet here so that we can drink whenever we want. And she'll give us further instructions later."

"Why are we here?" I whispered.

"She said something like 're-education', that we would be part of the economic revolution. But I didn't really understand what she meant."

I tried to pick up my head from the mattress, but I got dizzy and put it down again.

"Did they give out food?" I asked Seyoung.

"No, the registration lady said that provisions would arrive soon, and that we should wait patiently."

Seyoung stroked my forehead. "You are freezing. Should I bring you water? That's all we have here for now."

"Yes, I think that would help," I said thankfully.

Seyoung left the room and came back in a few minutes with an enamel bowl in her hand that looked like it had once been round, before something had crushed it. "Drink!" she commanded.

"There's no mug or other container?" I asked her quietly so that the two women wouldn't hear me.

"No, and she almost didn't give me this. Only when I said that you didn't manage to get up because you were so wiped out did she agree for me to take this container to you that we all had drunk from." Seyoung said these things as if she had already gotten used to drinking like that. I decided that maybe it was better to drink and recover, and try to understand what was happening here. I drank all the water in the container in one gulp.

"What else is here, and what are they going to do with us?" I asked Seyoung, hoping she would be able to explain everything.

"They said nothing besides about the registrations and the instructions I told you about," she answered. "No one knows what they'll do with us and when they'll return us to the village. In the meantime, they told us to wait for a food delivery, and divided us into two rooms."

I sat down and held my heavy head. Suddenly I remembered: "Where is Deshi?" and raised my voice in panic. "Have you seen him?"

"Deshi is in the other room. It seems that he also fell asleep. When you fainted, he just kept crying, and the registration lady pushed him into the room and screamed at him to calm down immediately."

I looked around. There were children sleeping on mattresses, and some sitting in a circle trying to understand how they had gotten there. I got up slowly so as not to fall again, and I asked Seyoung to help me find Deshi. "I must find him and calm him down."

With tiny steps, we advanced to the other room, which was bigger. It too was empty except for Mao's picture, which was different from the one hanging in the room where we were sleeping. Also here there were children on mattresses scattered on the floor. I found Deshi sleeping all rolled up, and didn't want to wake him. I asked one of the kids to tell Deshi, as soon as he woke up, that I had come to see him, and that I was fine.

We returned to our room more quickly because Seyoung told me that the scary registration lady had informed them that we could not mingle with the other room, and had to wait in the room until the food arrived. It was already dark, and we could see the darkness in the little window in the room, and only then did I understand that almost a whole day had gone by since they had taken us, and we'd had nothing to eat.

In a period of time that I could not define exactly, but that I could sense because of the rumbles of my tummy, the truck arrived. We heard the squeal of the brakes, and I hoped that we would receive a warm, nutritious meal. The registration lady stuck her head into the room and asked for some children to come and help. Seyoung and a few other friends joined me, and we went with her to the entrance.

"Help unpack the boxes of food!" she commanded in a threatening voice, and we stood behind the truck and waited for the driver to pass us the boxes. When I stretched my arms out toward the truck, I managed to see the face of the driver who had given me the box. The box was hot, and despite its weight, it was pleasant to hold and put near my body. I tried to catch the eye of the driver; maybe I could explain to him that I wasn't supposed to be there, that he had to take me back to the village. But the driver turned his back immediately after the box got to my hand, and I didn't manage to say anything. I could only see a large round mole on his cheek, out of which grew several long black hairs. I remembered this identifying mark when my fate led me to find my future.

***

The children of the night did not sleep at night; the night was their sign of life. It woke up all their senses, and made them flow with life.

Darkness fell for the first time on the children's house, and no child slept. But there were children who cried, and their crying was agonizing, crying of abandonment, crying of children who did not know what would happen to them. I was silent so that my voice wouldn't be lost in the cacophony of screams that made it impossible to sleep.

"Go to sleep!" The first command sounded like a battle cry, and indeed the first night was like a battlefield. "Stop crying right now!" came the voice of the registration lady, followed by that of Ms. Ushi-He who screamed, "Don't make us punish you already on the first night." I looked at them shrieking, at them and at the crying children, and I felt sorry for all of them: I felt sorry for the miserable children who had been seized from their homes and felt lost, and I felt sorry for the women who had lost their humanity. Only for myself, I did not cry that night. I still believed that all that would end soon for me.

The first days passed in confusion and uncertainty. Gradually, we understood that we would have to stay in that place until they found a solution for us, and in the meantime, it would be best if we didn't make the two women angry. Food came only once a day, and for many hours, we tried to escape by sleeping. The water faucet was in the hallway between the rooms, and we all drank from the same deep and misshapen container. Deshi had already gotten used to sleeping in the room with other boys, and I observed him every day and asked how he was.

Though there was a yard outside, they didn't let us go out to play or walk around. When we took the boxes of food, I saw a piece of metal equipment in the yard that looked like the swings that we had in the center of the village. I wondered if they would let us go out and play on them, but we never got to enjoy innocent child's play. Though we continued to sleep during the day, at night we were not allowed out.

Since we ate once a day, I tried to eat as much as I could so I wouldn't feel hungry the rest of the day. Every day they brought us the same thing: a cube of rice wrapped in a banana leaf that we opened and ate out of. Besides that, we each received an ear of corn or a potato, one each. The only extra serving we could get was rice.

***

In the children's home, there was one washroom with two pits for toilets. Sometimes we stood in line for so long that there were those who did not manage to hold it in, especially the younger ones. There was no shower. We washed ourselves using the drinking container. The children helped each other. The stench grew from day to day, particularly in the rooms where we slept. When one of the children did not get to the pit in time, he had to walk around without pants until his pants dried. The older girls washed the soiled clothes of the little ones.

The days passed slowly, the boredom was unbearable, and every day I hoped that my mother would come to get me. One night, I was lying down next to Seyoung while she tried to make shadow figures on the wall with her fingers. "Here is a wolf howling on the hill, chasing away a butterfly," she said, twisting her fingers to create first a wolf, and then a butterfly.

All of a sudden, I longed for the scent of my mother, the scent of laundry and sweat that I loved so much. I wanted Seyoung to make a silhouette of my mother, so that I could look at her again, at her soft hands that always arranged my hair, at her eyes that spoke and sang to me. "Seyoung," I said quietly, "I wanted to tell you that if my mother comes to get me, it will be hard for me to leave you, but I know that you are strong and will be okay until they come to get you." I was quiet for a moment and then continued. "It is Deshi that I am afraid to leave by himself. What will happen if they don't let me take him with me? How will he manage? If they don't let my mother take him too?" I pleaded with her, "Please help him."

Seyoung didn't answer and continued to make shadows on the wall, and for the first time since we had arrived at that place, I started to cry. After a while, I stopped crying, and from that moment, I didn't talk to her again about leaving.

***

One morning, Seyoung shook me with a heart-rending scream that echoed in the room like a lamentation, a cry that I had heard several times in our village. Little Anchi, who was sleeping next to the wall, looked blue and pretty. She was all curled up around herself like a snail.

Ms. Ushi-He arrived to the room out of breath and tried to wake Anchi with resounding slaps on her cheeks, but the girl didn't move, except for her head that jiggled from each smack. "Run and call my assistant," she yelled at me when she saw me standing there. "Her room is at the end of the hallway." I ran fast to the hallway that we were forbidden to walk in. I knocked on all the doors and tried to open each one, until I reached the last door, which was open, and there I saw the registration lady sitting on a raised bed holding something in her hand, that I later understood was a book.

"Come fast!" I yelled at her, breathlessly. "Ms. Ushi-He asked that I call you." The registration lady asked no questions, and ran after me to our room.

When we arrived, the children were outside the room, and I stayed with them when the registration lady went in. In a short time, a uniformed police officer arrived, and took our dead friend, wrapped in a sheet.

I had seen her on the truck that had brought us, and later in the large room on the day we arrived, withdrawn into herself. When she didn't talk, I thought she was shy, and I didn't notice that she had no friends. Sadness filled my heart, and nausea gripped me. Anchi always slept alone on the mattress, no one slept beside her to warm her. That's how I explained her death to myself because I couldn't come up with any other explanation.

That was the first time I had seen someone dead. I still didn't understand the meaning of loss, but I did understand that it was something horrible. During the day I could feel how well I understood, my whole body hurt, and I felt my muscles contracting. I started to whine. I cried because of the pain, I cried because I didn't understand what they would do with Anchi, I cried because I wanted my mother to come and hug me. Seyoung continued shouting explanations that I didn't manage to understand, and maybe I didn't hear because I was listening only to myself begging someone to come help her. Suddenly I panicked that my fate would be the same, that I would also die in that place without my parents, that I would also end my life curled up into myself.

Because of the pain in my muscles, I had the feeling that all the blood was emptying from my body. I felt my stomach turn as if it were kneading dough, but the dough was actually my internal organs. Then the pain went to my head, and this was a sharp pain that forced me to stop crying and take a deep breath. I looked for Seyoung, I wished she would come and hug me. I wanted the feeling to stop that I was losing my body, that hurt me so much, that someone needed to help me. I called her, and even though she was so close, she didn't hear me. She was on her knees and looked like a demon had gotten inside of her. She mumbled words that though they came out of her mouth, seemed as if they were not hers. I decided to go find Deshi in the hope that the search would distract me from the pain. With strength that I didn't know I had, I got up and headed for the door, and in the background, I heard the commotion in the room.

A little after the policeman effortlessly put Anchi's beautiful little sheet-wrapped body on his back and carried her away, Ms. Ushi-He gathered us into the large hall, and asked that we sit close to the wall. The wall was cold because it was already autumn. We didn't have any clothes that were right for the season, there were no heaters in the home, and therefore we clung to one another. Ms. Ushi-He told us what we already knew. "We lost a girl today. I hope that you can accept that, because that's life. Whoever isn't strong enough, sometimes doesn't survive," she said. Then she sat down in a chair. "I asked for blankets for you, and they promised me that the shipment would arrive soon," she said quietly. That made us happy, and at that time we believed that the blankets would indeed arrive. When they did arrive, it turned out that there were only enough for half the children, and thus we were forced to sleep in pairs.

During the first nights, I was near Seyoung, and it was hard for me to fall asleep. Her pungent odor penetrated my nostrils and nauseated me. I was ashamed to tell her that, because I figured that she probably had a problem with my odor, even though she always fell asleep right away. As time passed, I got used to the smells and the farewells from the children who didn't wake up. And as time passed, I hated that place more and more. I hated the walls that enclosed us, that prevented us from returning to our parents and our happy lives. I hated the principal and her assistant, who everyday would tell us how many of us had made it. The empty walls increased my longing for the colors at home, and the cold that prevented us from moving freely and forced us to warm each other reminded me of my mother's warm breast. The stabs of cold spread in my chest: it was painful to remember my mother picking me up, hugging me and singing.

The memories tortured me, the odors around were difficult to bear, sour nauseating odors that caused all of us to lose hope. The pathetic food, the cold treatment, the dirt that stuck to us that we couldn't remove---we never got used to these things. I had no idea how far I was from our village and from my parents, and there was not a day that I didn't pray that my mother would come and take me home. Deshi had already made friends with several boys in his room, and I felt that he needed my support less and less, until the day that he was burning with fever and mumbled my name, and Ms. Ushi-He agreed for me to sleep beside him to calm him. I didn't close my eyes the whole night. I wet the blanket a little with water from the drinking container, and I wiped it on his thin body, in the hopes of cooling him down. I remembered that that was how my mother took care of my father when he was sick and feverous. Ms. Ushi-He and the registration lady would come every once in a while to check on Deshi. They also didn't like finding dead children, and at that time, I didn't know that they could save them, just as I didn't know why they were dying.

Deshi's entire body trembled, and I hugged him in my arms, and sang a song that I remembered. The children gathered around us, and only then did I realized that that was the first time that someone had sung a song since we had arrived. When Ms. Ushi-He came in, I stopped immediately. "No, that's okay," she said. "Continue."

Get Up!

Our routine was dreadful, and we had no way of getting used to it. It was very hard for us to eat just once a day, and clean our bodies just once a week. When we finally managed to fall asleep at night, our morning would begin with a scream from the registration lady: "Get up!" I thought that in time she would soften the wake-up call by replacing the shout "Get up" with a shout "Good morning", and that way there would at least be hope that the morning would be good, but every day I was proven wrong all over again.

"Get up!" --- at the sound of the scream, everyone sat up in their bed and hastened to get up. Even after the first days, they still hadn't found us anything to do, and we didn't do very much. Besides entering the large hall to receive instructions, which were exactly the same instructions as the day before, we did nothing. One morning, after another child had died at night, two doctors came in to check us. We left the room and gathered in the large hall.

"Call everyone to come to the doctor for an examination, and go in to him one at a time," commanded Ms. Ushi-He. The doctors wanted to examine everyone, and they were forced to remain the entire day in order to see all the children.

When I entered the room that had been made into the

examination room, the registration lady introduced me by my name and immediately looked at me and said: "Don't start with that talk of your mother coming to take you home; the doctors have no time for your nonsense."

I stared at her and imagined my little hands reaching up to her thick neck, and pressing it with all the strength I had left. The registration lady's face turned red and then blue, the same color as the dead Anchi's face, and she dropped to the floor with a thud.

"Get undressed now!" yelled the registration lady. "Stop dreaming!"

I looked down and took off my clothes, the whole time hugging myself in an attempt to warm up. The doctor asked me to lie down on the mattresses, and then he shined his light into my eyes. He pressed my stomach in a few places, and since the presses tickled me, I laughed.

The doctor looked at me and said: "A healthy girl, very healthy." He sounded very pleased, and I continued smiling.

"You just need to eat a little more," he said and smiled too, but that was exactly when I felt my smile fade and I started to cry. I couldn't control the tears that streamed down my cheeks.

"Quiet, Ming, act like a big girl," said the registration lady said, but I couldn't stop.

The doctor, who didn't understand what had happened to me all of a sudden, tried to calm me and talked to me gently.

"Are you hungry?" he asked.

I shook my head no, because I couldn't get a word out of my mouth.

"What happened, Ming, tell me," the doctor said, trying to understand.

"I am a firstborn," I managed to say between sobs, but he

apparently didn't hear, because he asked again: "What happened to you?"

At that moment, the registration lady got up and pounced toward me. She grabbed my right arm, picked me up from the mattress, and with her other hand, grabbed my clothes that were on the side in a pile, opened the door and pushed me out. When I landed on the floor, she threw my clothes at me and said through clenched teeth, "You are not behaving properly, and you'll be punished for it."

I stayed on the frozen floor and cried. I cried so hard, that the other doctor came out of the little room to see what had happened. He bent down to me. "We understand that you have not been eating enough," he said quietly. "We will ask that they bring more food here so that you won't be weak and will have the strength to play. I didn't stop crying. I was afraid to tell him that I wasn't crying about food, that I wanted to explain my situation to them and ask them to take me away from here, but my fear of the registration lady prevented me from doing so.

The sound of my weeping reached the ears of Ms. Ushi-He, and she arrived in quick steps, stood above me, and in her strong voice said: "Get dressed immediately and return to the large hall." She continued standing, and I got dressed as quickly as possible, and crawling on all fours, I returned to the room. I had no strength or desire to stand on my feet.

"What are you, a dog?" asked Ms. Ushi-He who walked after me. "Get on your feet right now."

But I said nothing and continued to crawl to the hall entrance. There, before I raised my head to see the children waiting inside, I felt a kick in the butt that threw me inside.

Many years later, when I had grown up and the children's

home was a faraway memory, I understood that what I had felt then was humiliation. Every time I thought of the children's home, and it was almost every day of my life, I understood that these feelings didn't break my body or my soul, but quite the opposite. They strengthened me and gave me the power to continue to take it all, to hold out and prove to everyone that in the end I would manage to return to the village.

***

Every afternoon the truck would arrive, and all of us went out to help lug in the boxes. Not everyone was required for the task, but all the children enjoyed going outside to breathe a little fresh air and look around at the flat landscape, and the metal playground equipment that we never got to play with. The children who took the boxes did it very slowly so that our limited time outside would last as long as possible. A few days after the doctors' visit, we went out to the truck, and this time all the children took a box. We immediately understood that there were more boxes this time, but that evening's food serving was identical to what had been served on the previous days: a rice cube wrapped in a boiled banana leaf. Ms. Ushi-He and the registration lady served us the food in the large hall, and we sat on the cold floor to eat. Since the doctors' visit, every time I was in that room with Ms. Ushi-He or the registration lady, I looked down. The next morning, the registration lady entered the room with her usual scream "Get up", but this time, we were surprised to hear her screech another command: "and right away to the large hall."

When we woke up, we opened our eyes and tried to look alert; but most of us did everything we could to hold on to our dreams. As always, we paraded sleepily to the large hall, but this time, a big surprise was waiting for us. "From now on," announced Ms. Ushi-He, "every morning, you'll receive another portion of rice and vegetables, per the doctor's orders. You all must eat, so that you'll be strong enough." Shouts of happiness were heard in the room, and I didn't know if that was because the children were really hungry, or because they had added another activity to our miserable, boring routine that would take up about an hour per day.

Seyoung and I hugged each other as if we had just been told that our entire lives were about to change. Our lives did change, but not enough to shake the feeling of stagnation that had been holding me since the incident with the doctors. The additional meal indeed improved the physical condition of some of the children. Deshi, who still often cried in my arms, suddenly felt heavy. I eventually realized that he had grown.

The idleness between the morning and evening meals was unbearable. Most of the time the children slept because they had found no other way to pass the time, and every time that someone started crying out loud, the ladies would come into the room and make clear that crying would not help, but would only lead to unnecessary punishments.

Gradually we learned to stifle the crying. In addition, every day, good and gentle Seyoung would try to bring in a few more children to the fantasy game that we played. The rules were simple: someone said a sentence and the others continued, each one in turn, until a fantasy story was made up that was usually not logical. The only rule was that you couldn't speak about the village or the people we knew there. Every day, we sailed to faraway places, limited only by our imagination.

***

The day we received the first additional meal in the morning, we returned to the room. Seyoung sat on the floor and asked us to sit in a circle. "I'm starting a story, and each of you will add to it, until we have a long story."

She waited until everyone was sitting, and enthusiastically encouraged anyone who was a little afraid of the new game, and it quickly became our favorite game at the children's home. After she lost patience and wanted to start, Seyoung raised her voice a little and said: "One day, Feng woke up and went out to work in the fields as he did every morning at his children's home."

I sat to the left of Seyoung and felt her touch my knee and signal for me to continue. I sat up straight and said: "Feng told his good friend Chong that the day before, when he was ploughing the land, he had found a chest full of treasure." I was so proud of myself for having come up with a sentence that was so full of mystery, I even smiled a bit.

Dong-Hu, who was sitting next to me, understood that now it was his turn. He got up on his long, thin legs that were barely able to hold his clumsy body, and announced in a dramatic voice: "In the chest were a hunting rifle and a notebook with maps marked with the escape route…" Dong-Hu finished his sentence merrily and sat down, while everyone laughed and clapped for him like at the end of a show.

Hui asked if he had to get up, and Seyoung said that we would play the game sitting down, except for Dong-Hu who was to get up every time it was his turn. Everyone laughed, laughter of release that for a moment made everyone forget our tormented existence at the children's home. We sailed to our world of imagination and games, the world of the lost children. Hu-Vi, in a wheezy voice, continued: "Feng and Chong decided to go out and follow the first map looking for the escape route, if they see it, they'll fire a shot with the rifle…" Her squeaks turned into a whisper so she wouldn't be heard outside the room.

Little Dishi, who seemed to have been very excited, was deep in contemplation for a moment, and then continued the story: "They shook hands and went on a journey beyond the mountains." He also whispered as if he had said something forbidden.

Jiali, who was sitting next to him, asked if he had finished and if it was her turn to speak. Everyone answered together impatiently: "Speak, speak!" and she continued: "From afar they saw a village, and walked toward it." Her mouth stayed open as if she wanted to continue talking, but we were already used to her mouth always being open in a strange way.

Seyoung stopped the story for a moment and asked that whoever finished speaking touch the knee of the person sitting next to him, "so that we don't have to ask questions, and don't need to interrupt the story." Seyoung's firmness was new to me, and caused me to see her with great appreciation.

Liang, whose messy hair gave him a babyish look, sat silently the whole time, as if he didn't want to disappoint the audience, and immediately continued: "In the village, they didn't let them sleep in any of the sheds, and they sat and cried until some good person let them into his house and gave them tea and rice." Even before he had said the last word, he touched the knee of Sying, who continued immediately, so as not to be the one who stopped the flow of the story. "They showed him the map, they did it because he was a good man, and after that they told him where they had come from."

Zhu started to talk when he felt the touch on his knee, but I immediately noticed that he stuttered. Maybe he found it hard to keep up with the flow of thoughts, and felt pressured having to quickly make up and say a sentence that minute, or maybe he always stuttered, and I just had never noticed. "They gave the good man their gun," he said quickly. Zhu did not touch Kiew's knee, and she didn't continue. For a minute, it was quiet, and then Zhu continued: "and they thanked him for the help."

That was the end of the circle, and Kiew touched Seyoung's knee without trying to say a sentence herself. We didn't understand if we had finished the story, and all of us waited in suspense for Seyoung to speak. Indeed, Seyoung didn't disappoint us, and quickly provided a sentence, as if she had been thinking about it the whole time. "They walked a few days until they arrived at a place where they wouldn't be discovered."

I tensed up a bit and tried to quickly come up with a sentence that would also be interesting. I sat up straight and said, "They sat and thought and checked the maps again, and ultimately decided to continue walking in order to find a place that was better and farther away." I touched Dong-Hu's knee, and I was happy with my short sentence this turn.

Dong-Hu stood up again. He folded his arms behind his back, and said in a loud, clear voice: "The entire way they tried to guess what would be at the new place they would get to, and if everything would work out okay."

Hui didn't wait for Dong-Hu to sit down and touch her knee, and with bated breath, hurried to continue the story: "They stopped for the night in another place, and went to sleep very tired." Hui's blunt nose always looked to me as if he had been hit when he was a baby, but I never asked her about it.

Dishi, whose turn it was, shot out his sentence as if wanting his turn to be over quickly. "They discovered that the place they had arrived at was full of good people."

Jiali, the most relaxed of the children, took a deep breath through her open mouth and returned the relaxed pace of the story. "They decided to go back to the field where they worked and bring more friends."

Liang continued speaking at Dishi's pace: "They returned to the village, but no one believed them, and everyone was afraid to come with them."

Sying, who was a good-looking boy, leaned back on his hands, either from fatigue or boredom, and spoke: "They weren't very sorry, and decided to run back to the new place they had discovered."

It was again Zhu's turn, and this time he filled his lungs with air, and said his sentence in a lighter stutter: "On the way they met a tiger, and the tiger didn't devour them, but joined them to help them."

Seyoung didn't wait for Chang to touch her, and burst out with her sentence: "In the end, they managed to get to the nice place where all the people were good."

I, who was already tired of the story, and of sitting in an uncomfortable position, concluded: "And that's the end of the story."

The Harvest

Life took another turn, and fate came back to mislead me when one morning the masculine Ms. Ushi-He announced with her usual shrieks that we would be driven every morning to work in the rice fields of the neighboring villages, and thus we would contribute to our great developing country. Of course, we were very happy to hear that our daily schedule had finally changed, but we couldn't have imagined how much we would end up longing for the boring routine and our fantasy games.

The next morning, four trucks arrived that were smaller than the ones that had brought us to the children's home. The children from each room were divided into two groups. My name was on the first list, and Seyoung's name was on the second. I got on the truck and tried to see if Seyoung would also get on a truck. The trucks started to drive, and for some reason I had the idea that maybe my truck would return to the village, and I felt sorry for Seyoung and Deshi. At the end of the long ride, we stopped next to a few sheds that were larger than the houses in the village. A few men approached the truck and asked us to get off.

They seemed different from the groups of men that I had seen when I had visited my father in the fields. Not only were they stockier, and maybe shorter, their features weren't pleasant like those of the men I remembered from my village. For a moment I thought that maybe my memory was deceiving me, or that I had grown up and so the men seemed shorter to me. Their faces were scorched by the sun, and their lips were swollen and black, which added to their crude and frightening look. We followed them silently; we no longer had the strength to cry. We had learned that weeping did not change anything, and it mostly just wore us out.

After walking a few minutes, we got to the rice fields. There were also rice fields in my village. They had always looked nice to me, tidy, pleasant, and green. The rice fields we were facing were much bigger, almost endless. For a moment, it was nice to stand and look at this stunning landscape.

"Dear children," one of the men said, "you have arrived during the season where we are still growing the rice. Form lines and we will show you how to pick the plants that bother the rice within the paddies."[1]

The men divided us into smaller groups, and I walked with three other girls behind a particularly short man. We watched him walk into the swamp, and then followed. He was wearing knee-high rubber boots, and we were wearing fabric shoes that we had received from the children's home after we had outgrown the shoes we had worn when we first came in from the village. We followed him into the cold water and saw how he plunged his hands into the water, and pulled the leaves out from the root. Since we had already seen rice harvested in our village, and were familiar with the method used for removing the plants that grew in the water alongside the rice,

---

1   Most rice grows in fields called "paddies", shallow puddles about 15 cm deep.

the explanations were short. We spread out around him, and started to pick the weeds.

We returned to the sheds to get bags that we hung on our shoulders with leather straps, and returned to the fields to continue picking weeds. We were wet, and very cold, but the first day was very exciting because we enjoyed being away from the children's home; we were thrilled by the new activity, but mainly because the men that we worked with did not raise their voices at us like Ms. Ushi-He and the registration lady. I looked for an opportunity to talk with one of the men. I had to ask him what he knew of our fate. I had to find an opportunity to tell him that I was there by mistake, and that he should help me return to the village, because my mother would never manage to find this place. But then I remembered the incident with the doctor, and decided to wait a bit, and not ask just yet.

When the sun went down, my legs were completely frozen and I couldn't feel them at all. I still smiled because I saw the sun and felt that fate was hinting to me that something was about to change. I so wanted to feel that something good would happen that the fear of Ms. Ushi-He disappeared for a few minutes. On the way back to the truck, I approached the short man and said to him with a big smile, "Good night, mister."

"Good night. Sleep well because tomorrow will be harder," he answered with a smile.

Encouraged by the look of his smile, I got closer to him, but he moved back a little. "I must tell you something," I said quickly. "You must help me. I am a firstborn, not one of the children of the night, they took me here by mistake, I want to return to the village…" He looked at me for a moment and asked, "Then why didn't they come to take you?" I looked down because I didn't have an answer, and I really didn't understand why my mother hadn't come yet. Why was it taking her so long to come here and bring me home? I felt my heart beat quickly and everything around me started to spin.

"Move it!" the short man said. "Get on the truck, maybe tomorrow they'll come to get you." I walked back to the truck and felt my chest open and let my heart beat outside my body. The feeling that my heart was pounding outside my body would return in the future when I was in the midst of another distressful situation.

***

In the subsequent days, the trucks arrived immediately after breakfast. I asked the girls in Seyoung's group to switch with me in the truck, but everyone was afraid. Every morning Seyoung and I would separate for the hours of work. The excitement of the first day was replaced with cold blisters on our feet, and bleeding scratches on our hands. From the moment we arrived at the field until sunset, we worked. They didn't let us rest unless we asked to go to the bathroom, and then we were forced to move far away from the field and the water.

I didn't know how much time had passed since we had started to work in the fields, but I noticed that we had already seeded twice and harvested three times. In our village, they would seed and harvest the rice just once a year, but the fields here were different. Maybe the weather was different or maybe it was because of the way we worked, or the type of irrigation. In any case, I didn't know and I didn't ask.

I always felt the time that had passed: my hands hurt, my face was scorched by the sun or chapped by the cold, the silence all around us during the difficult work caused us to become distanced from one another, to slowly submerge into and be obliterated by the endless rice fields. I didn't understand what they meant when they explained to me that I was part of the revolution. I only understood what I had to do, and that the principal and her assistant were replaced by different guards during work.

The work became routine, a difficult and painful routine. We had already managed to see the rice grow, and to drain the water from the paddies to facilitate the harvest. We harvested the dry rice, threshed it to separate the grains, and we even learned a better method to remove the hulls. We had already been through the entire life cycle of rice several times, and continued to work from morning to evening. We returned so tired that we stopped speaking to each other. After supper, we hurried to get into bed, and fell asleep the moment our heads hit the mattresses. If the objective was for us to lose our identities, it had almost been achieved. Only the longing for my parents filled me with hope that the end was near.

***

Sometimes Seyoung would ask to play a short fantasy game. "Just one sentence each," she would beg me every time, "until we fall asleep." On especially sad nights, we played, a few kids together, and everyone quickly said his sentence so that we could go to sleep quickly. The dialogs always led someone somewhere else. Someone always escaped alone or with a group. We never played the game and ended up staying at the children's home. We always fled to a better place.

In the winter, it was hard to set foot in the flooded paddies.

The cold water penetrated the plastic bags that we tied over our feet, and our hands froze while we worked. The period between the harvest and the next planting started in mid-winter, and we needed to clean the paddies of the weeds that tried to grow there in the interim. Years later, when I had the opportunity to hold my hands under a stream of warm water for more than an hour, I'd think of my frozen clenched hands in the rice fields.

In the summer, the work in the blazing sun was no less harsh and painful. Though they provided us with wide straw hats, the heat was intense, and nothing prevented the sun from scorching every part of our bodies. However, it wasn't just our bodies that burned as a result of our backbreaking work, but also our souls, which we had brought with us from the village as children. We lived the life cycle of the fields, and observed all that beauty without being able to rejoice in it, without being able to be moved by the buds or maturing of the plants. We worked every day, regardless of the weather.

Time marched on, and every night, when I looked at Seyoung before we went to sleep, I knew that I was growing. Seyoung was my mirror during all the years of my adolescence in the children's home. She was my mirror to the physical changes that took place in me, the femininity that tried to find its place in my body, to the hard work in the fields; my mirror to the time passing by.

I first noticed the signs that she was growing up. Suddenly I saw that her nipples stood out under the fabric of her shirt, and I knew that we were maturing, that time had not stopped, and that my mother still had not arrived. We had already been at the children's house at least four years, though I had no way of knowing exactly how much time had passed. I saw Seyoung grow right before my eyes, and when I looked at my body, I noticed that my breasts had grown and I had underarm and pubic hair.

Every day in the fields, when I asked the men to go to the bathroom, another girl would join me so I wouldn't be alone. One afternoon, I felt the fatigue overwhelm me and I came up with the idea of asking for a break just to rest a little. Hu-Vi joined me and together we crossed the water and continued toward the houses. We found a low place that was mostly hidden, put down our bags, and she immediately pulled down her pants and sat down. I lay down on the ground and closed my eyes to keep out the sun, gathering strength to get through the day.

Hu-Vi finished what she had to do and put the bag back on her shoulder. I asked her to wait a few minutes so that I could rest, but she refused, and ran back quickly. I hurried after her, barely catching up, and we returned to the waterlogged fields. I continued to work with great difficulty. My legs hurt me in the water, I had the feeling that they were sinking deeply into the water, and I did not manage to pick them up so that I could move forward. My eyes filled with tears, but my hands continued to harvest automatically from within the water.

I was in deep despair. I had the feeling that I would stay there forever, that if until that day my mother had not come, she apparently never would come. I fell to my knees, and heard the short man yell at me to get up. I had no energy, and was already thinking of giving up, breaking, stop being strong, and losing the battle over returning to the village. I fell into the water, and only when my face was flushed with the cold water did my brain clear and I woke up in a panic. I got up, looked around, and knew that I had to take charge of my fate. I decided to run away.

***

On the way back in the truck, I sat withdrawn into myself. Thoughts ran through my head, and I didn't manage to make sense of them. Was it better to run away at sunset, or maybe in the afternoon? Should I hide in one of the houses, or maybe stay on the truck? I had to check out all the possibilities, I couldn't make mistakes.

When I entered the children's home, exactly at suppertime, I looked for Seyoung to share my thoughts with her. I started to tell her what had happened to me that day, and then I remembered that Hu-Vi had refused to wait a bit so that I could rest. I got up from my place, and marched toward her. She was sitting on the floor, and in her hand was a banana leaf with rice. I looked at it from above and kicked her hand. The leaf flew into the air and fell onto the floor, and she screamed in pain and looked up at me.

"Would it have been so difficult for you to wait a little while so that I could rest?" I screamed with intensity I didn't know I had. "I just wanted to gather a bit of strength so that I could continue," I said in pain. "Why couldn't you act like a friend and be considerate of me? Why were you in such a rush to get back? What, was someone waiting for us here?!" Hu-Vi looked at me expressionless, and then she burst into tears.

Your tears don't impress me at all," I screamed at her. "You are so selfish!" and then I felt the registration lady grab my hand and pull me back. "Get out of here at once and go to your room! You're not getting any supper tonight."

When I got to the room, I lay down on my mattress and stared at the ceiling. Within the confusion of thoughts, I understood what I already knew: that a long time had gone by and that my mother would never come. Fate was hinting that it was time to take control of the situation. I focused completely on the thoughts of escaping from the field, and I tried to make plans in my head. But then everyone returned, and Seyoung lay down next to me. "What happened to you?" she whispered quietly. "I've never seen you like that."

"Why couldn't she just let me rest a bit? Why was it so hard for her to wait for me for a little while?" I tried to explain to Seyoung what I had gone through, but I understood that my outburst had been over the top. I felt the despair take control of me and cause me to speak and behave in a way that was not typical of me. But that desperation also helped me decide it was time to run away. I didn't share this secret with Seyoung. She wasn't in the same group as me anyway, and I didn't trust anyone anymore. I had nothing to lose, since such a long time had passed and no one had come to take me, it was better that I try to return alone. This time I decided not to submit to my fate but to try and change it.

***

The next morning, on the way to the large hall, Ms. Ushi-He called me. "What is the meaning of this behavior of yours? Either you pull yourself together immediately, or you will be punished," she said decisively. I looked down and didn't answer. "Go eat," she said. "And I'm warning you!" I went into the hall, and for a moment, I felt no need to apologize to Hu-Vi. She had stolen precious minutes of rest from me, and I couldn't forgive her. I sat next to Seyoung and started to eat. Seyoung stroked my hair and said, "Ming, what's happening to you? You're changing." I chuckled to myself, and had no more compassion.

On the way to the fields, I tried not to look at Hu-Vi, and I decided to concentrate on preparing my escape plan. During the course of the entire day, I surveyed the area and observed what went on. I examined especially carefully the area of the sheds, and checked whether it was possible to hide near them. I tried to calculate the distance from the fields to the closest hills, in case I decided to run. I thought about the time it takes us to get back to the trucks, and I decided that that was when to do it, though I took into account the fact that after a day's work I would be tired and hungry. I looked at the men and studied what they did from the time work ended until we got onto the buses back to the children's home.

At night, I tried to force myself to stay awake, so that I would be able to think of all the details. My first conclusion was that I should hide food in my clothes so that I would have provisions for the first night of the escape, when I was hiding. The plan was to flee as everyone was getting on the trucks, and I hoped that I would manage to go through with it. This was when, the sun had already set, the men were facing the houses, and we were getting on the buses without being told to do so. I was encouraged by the thought, and even more by the light of the moon that came into the room through the little window, so that I could see the figure of Mao looking at me as if reading my thoughts.

Only one thing troubled me and made it difficult for me to do what I wanted to do: the fear that my mother would arrive and I wouldn't be there. But desperation defeated fear, and my desire to escape was intensifying. I decided not to act hastily, and for a few days, I checked over and over again the steps I would take. I knew that if I were caught trying to escape, the punishment would be extremely harsh.

The thoughts about the difficulty of the work and the physical pain were pushed aside. I concentrated completely on planning the escape, and that helped me get through each day. The plan had already been devised, and all I had to do was collect food for a few days without anyone noticing. Every day of planning ended with a prayer that either my mother would arrive or I would succeed in escaping.

The next day, on the way to the fields, I thought that maybe it was my last day there. Maybe I would ask Hu-Vi for forgiveness for the kick and for my bad behavior, I thought. Ultimately, I decided that that was liable to disrupt my plans because maybe she wouldn't understand why I was apologizing after so many days of our ignoring each other. And maybe she would suddenly notice that I hadn't gotten onto the truck, and she would yell to the men that I had run away. I decided to keep quiet, even though I didn't want to leave her like that, when we were still angry with each other.

The trucks brought us to the fields. I did not exchange a word with any of my friends, and I did not look the men in the eye. I did everything I possibly could to not call attention to myself. Once, a long time ago, I saw a chameleon in my house in the village, and my father told me that there were chameleons that change their colors, and that's how they protect themselves from predators. I very much wanted to be such a chameleon, to be able to change color and blend in with the colors of the fields. All day I worked at a faster pace than usual, and didn't rest for a second. I didn't even ask to go to the bathroom, the main thing was to remain unnoticed.

The sun beat down on our heads; I understood that the day was moving along, and I could feel my heart pounding. I tried not to have my pants pocket get wet, because I had put two portions of rice in it from yesterday's supper as food for the first day of my escape.

The sun had set, indicating that it was time to finish up and return the bags to the warehouse, which caused me great excitement at the thought that I was going to run away. Everyone walked together, but I walked alone at the side, and looked around to make sure that the men were heading toward their hut, and the children were walking toward the truck. I walked slowly so I would be last. Some of the children were already on the truck, and the men turned in the other direction.

I walked around and waited impatiently to see that everyone was heading toward the place from which we boarded the trucks. I breathed deeply and held my breath. I saw the men go into the hut, and then the moment came that I had been imagining for a very long time, the short moment that I had thought about every night since I had decided to escape. I stood in place to make sure that they were not looking at me. I ran quickly toward the hut without looking back, and crouched down behind it. I tried to return to breathing quietly when I heard the truck drive off. I heard the men's voices within the hut, and decided not to move from where I was until it was completely dark. Curled up on the damp ground, I waited for night to fall. The heat had dissipated, and when it became dark, a cool wind began to blow. I waited for night to fall the way I had waited for it during my childhood in the village. I waited to go out to freedom when the sun disappeared as if I was again disguised as a child of the night, and I wasn't at all afraid. I thought of my mother, of Seyoung, and of Deshi, wondering if I would ever see them again. I felt a small victory thanks to this moment, when I sat alone after a long period when I was never really alone, even though in the children's home I felt the most alone in the world.

Night came, the moon shone faintly. I was sorry that I hadn't waited for the full moon, but it was already too late, I had run away. I started to walk toward the fields in order to try to cross them and try my luck on the other side of them. My feet were again in the cold water. I could have escaped during the season where they dry the rice, but unfortunately, I hadn't thought of that either.

I walked, a lot, I had no idea for how long, but I could feel the heaviness in my legs. I wanted to already get to dry land, to get out of that never-ending swamp. While walking, I took out one of the banana leaves that contained a little rice, which I ate slowly, grain by grain. From afar, I saw a slight sparkle. I didn't manage to identify it, but it was a small light source, and I didn't think that I had gotten to a place where people lived.

I walked toward the little light, and when I got there, I saw that it was a metal pole, at the end of which was a round surface that could be stood on to observe the fields. There was a pole near the fields where we worked, and the men would climb it to see if an animal had come into the field. I decided to sit at this small observation station and rest awhile. I climbed on the post, hugged it with both legs, and before I had had time to think about what was going on with me, I fell asleep.

***

I woke up from the coldness of the post. It was still dark, and I decided to wait for sunlight before moving on. I couldn't fall asleep again. I tried to imagine what might have happened when the truck had returned without me. I hoped that Seyoung and Deshi wouldn't worry. For a moment I was sorry that I hadn't told them, I could have saved them from worrying. None of the others were important to me, but Seyoung was my best friend, and I was thinking that she would cry from the pain of not knowing what had happened to me.

I also felt bad for Deshi as I had promised him that I would take care of him. Though recently we hadn't spoken much at all, I noticed that he had matured and grown taller, and had suddenly turned in a sturdy boy. But I had given him my word. I swore quietly that when I arrived in the village, I would do everything I could to return to the children's home and bring him back.

Echo of a Scream

I remained on the round end surface of the post, still hugging the post. The morning was taking its own sweet time, without taking into consideration my prayers for morning light to help me see where I had gotten to. I gazed at the heavens above me and at the sky that was slowly clearing. Around me were green rice fields that from the height of the post appeared to be spread out and divided into large plots. I still hadn't seen any houses or people, and I decided to get down from my observation point and continue on my way.

I felt the hunger gnawing at me and my whole body was trembling. It wasn't shivering from cold, rather from something uncontrollable, the trembling of a frightened body in a foreign place, a body that as much as it longs to belong, is rejected. I got down from the post and looked around, but I wasn't able to figure out from which direction I had come, and I didn't know which way to go. All the rice fields seemed to me as if copied with amazing precision, and looking at them, I saw that I could have come from any direction. I chose a side and started to walk again within the puddles of the fields. The sun had already warmed me up, and walking in the water was easier.

I hoped to see something on the horizon, but there was

nothing else besides the fields. Time passed quickly, the pleasant sun warmed my body, and for a while I had the feeling that I had succeeded, that I was on my way. My feeling of freedom, all alone with myself, spread throughout my body and quickened the pace of my steps. I felt a shy little smile creep onto my lips. For the moment, I was in control of my fate, and I knew that the decision to flee had been courageous and right. I had no future in that horrible place, and had already lost hope that anyone would come and take me from there.

"I am walking to my freedom," was the mantra that I mumbled to myself, and I very much wanted to believe that that would happen. After a long walk, I could see several houses on the horizon. I turned toward them, and increased my pace until I heard the sound of my strained breathing. The rice fields around me seemed familiar, and suddenly I feared that I had already walked through those same fields. The closer I got, huffing and puffing, the more the huts I saw looked like the sheds of the men in the fields. I understood that I had retraced my steps.

I collapsed into the water in despair, and my labored breaths turned into howls. I refused to believe that all that walking had actually been in one big circle, and that I had returned right to where I had set out from, without even noticing. I was afraid, and the fear replaced the pace and the smile and the hope that I had had during the previous few hours.

With each breath, I was more and more afraid, but though the fear filled my entire body, it did not leave me when I breathed out. I needed my mother to wrap herself around me, as she had done at the hospital, when she gave birth to me. I needed my mother to take me from there. I turned my face to the sky and screamed, "Mother! Come already!" When I heard the return echo of the scream, I understood that there was no one else to hear me but myself.

Desperation returned and took control of me. I was hungry and my entire body was trembling. I continued walking toward the huts that I had already recognized. The children and the men were not there yet, and as I ran to the large shed, I formulated the cover story for my failed escape attempt in my head. I lay down behind the shed and decided to pretend I was sleeping. I surrendered to my fate that had not let me take charge of it. I waited for the sound of the trucks arriving. I heard the sound of an engine, but it was that of a small car, which the men soon came out of.

I remained lying on the ground, near the wall of the hut. The men came to the shed and opened the door, but still hadn't noticed me. I heard them talking loudly, but I didn't move. I was waiting in the same place, still trying to decide what I would tell everyone when they found me near the shed. I was so tired that I fell asleep, and when I woke up, I found it was already dark. I wondered what punishment I would receive from the principal and her assistant. I prepared myself to receive no food for a few days, as they had already punished some of the other children.

Finally, the trucks arrived and I heard the men go out to them. I jumped up too, and ran to the trucks when my friends were getting out. When they saw me, they yelled out my name and came toward me in a group.

"Where were you? We were worried! We thought they had kidnapped you!" Jiali yelled to me. I hugged her, shaking and crying, and at that moment, I decided what to tell everyone.

"I was kidnapped," I heard myself whisper to Jiali. "I was about to get on the truck, and someone put a bag over my head and pulled me. I heard you driving off, and didn't understand why you had left without me," I added with a trembling voice.

"The main thing is that you are okay," said Jiali excitedly. "The principal was boiling mad because she thought that you had run away," she continued, trying to release herself from my hug. I was imagining the two women turning red, with smoke coming out of their ears in their fury. I was so afraid that it was hard for me to breathe. I could feel hot liquid drip between my legs and run down to my feet. Slowly, my nose sensed a terrible odor of feces, and I understood that I had lost control over my body.

***

I felt them slapping my cheeks. I opened my eyes and saw everyone standing over me, including the men. Fear took control of me again. I closed my eyes and asked in my heart to be in a different place, and more than that, I wanted not to be, not to exist at all. Though this feeling was very stressful, my physical needs grew stronger at that moment, and since I stank so much, I had to get up.

The men asked a truck driver to wait and take me back to the children's home. I got on the truck, and I stood up for the entire ride, holding onto the bar. The way back seemed short, even though I really didn't want to get there. My tears flew in the wind that hit my face. They didn't stream down my cheeks. The smell of my feces nauseated me, but I didn't manage to vomit---apparently my body was already completely empty, and there was nothing else to go out of it; again I felt that it wasn't under my control. I felt that I had lost control of my body, of fate, and for the first time, also of my soul, which wanted to leave me.

I stood on the truck, swaying in place, and I only hoped that they would let me get washed so that the nausea would stop, but that didn't happen so fast. The sound of the truck returning brought the assistant principal to the gate, and she immediately took a good look at me, standing in the open part of the truck. I got off the truck, dragging my feet. She stood before me with arms folded and stared in anger. "You'd better have a pretty good explanation for what happened," she reprimanded. "You've angered everyone here."

I looked down and mumbled quietly, "I was kidnapped." The assistant principal sniffed the air and stepped backwards. "What's that smell?" she asked furiously. "Where were you mucking around?" I couldn't look up at her, and didn't really want to, so I just said: "I was so frightened, I soiled my pants." At that moment, a part of the assistant principal's personality that she had managed to hide very well over the years was revealed—she suddenly became human. I could see that her face was pretty, especially with her hair pulled back. "Go get cleaned up," she said in a softer voice. "After that, you'll tell me what happened." Later I found out that that had been a one-time display of humanity.

I was disgusted with myself, but I understood that no one else was going to clean me, and that I had to do it to stop my discomfort. I took off my clothes and saw that the results of my fear were smeared all over my body. It seemed like someone had drawn all over me with a brush dipped in feces. I filled the little container of water so many times that my hand hurt. Little by little I managed to clean off the traces of feces from my body, but the smell stuck to me for many days. When I had finished washing myself, I ran to the room to get clean clothes, and then I sat in the corridor and waited for the assistant principal.

The principal and her assistant came out of their rooms and stood in front of me. "Talk!" they commanded in one voice. My body had another attack of trembling in fear of what would happen to me as a result of my failed attempt to escape.

"I went with everyone to the truck and suddenly someone covered my face and I felt them pulling me back" – that was the beginning of the story, but I had no idea what the rest was. My whole body shook, my stomach contracted, and I felt the bile rise into my throat. I put my hand over my mouth in an attempt to keep myself from throwing up. The principal looked at me skeptically, but told me to go rinse my mouth and lie down in the room until I felt better. I went back to the water faucet to wash my mouth, and was glad I had been given time to organize the story I had made up. Though for now I had been saved from a beating, the shame I felt at what had happened to me in the field in front of everyone stayed with me for a very long time.

***

When I got to the room, I lay down on the mattress and fell asleep as soon as I closed my eyes. Seyoung woke me up by shaking me hard. Crying bitterly, she hugged me tight. "What happened, Ming? What happened?" she asked, her face covered with tears. "I didn't believe them when they said you had probably run away. You wouldn't do something like that without me, would you?" Later when I looked for her everywhere, I would remember that sentence.

I tried to get up, but I became nauseated again, and also

couldn't see through the tears. I hugged Seyoung and whispered quietly, "I was kidnapped." But I didn't continue because
I was afraid she would see that I was lying. "I'll tell you about it
later," I said quietly. "Right now I don't feel so well."

The rest of the children stood over me and looked at me.
I looked for Deshi among them, but I didn't see him. Despite
the distance that had been created between us at that time,
and the fact that he didn't need me anymore, at that moment
I felt that I needed his support, but he wasn't there to give it to
me. Seyoung asked everyone to let me rest, and I stayed in bed
the whole evening, not even getting up to eat. I wanted to plan
my story so it would be coherent, and have nothing that would
arouse suspicion that I was lying.

I decided to tell myself a story sentence by sentence, as we
had done in the room when we had just arrived at the children's home:

They covered my head and mouth.

They pulled me back and sat me on the ground.

I heard the trucks drive off, and after that, I sat for a long
time.

I couldn't yell.

They got me up and put me into a closed place, apparently
one of the sheds.

They kept my head covered, only lifting the covering only a
bit to allow me to drink water.

I heard two men speaking of how their plan had been a
success.

They said that they thought they had kidnapped a teenage
girl, and that that wouldn't work.

They decided to leave me near the shed while they went to
ask Hasipu, the senior worker what to do.

They took me out of the shed and left.

I stayed that way outside until the morning when the men came.

I was afraid it was them, so I stayed quiet until the children came.

I went over all these details in my head while I lay awake near Seyoung who fell asleep smiling. Apparently, she was so happy that I had returned and hadn't deserted her. I was envious that she could smile, and in my heart, I hoped that fate would also bring me smiles.

***

In the morning, when everyone was getting up, the assistant principal came to me and asked if I felt better.

"I am still nauseated," I answered quietly.

She stood over me, and with a soft, non-threatening look said: "Go eat. You didn't eat anything yesterday." I got up slowly so as not to get dizzy from hunger and weakness. "Today you are not going out to the fields," she said. "Instead of that, you will help with the cleaning work." I wanted to go to the fields to avoid the conversation, but it was clear to me that I could not.

I sat next to Seyoung and ate my rice. I managed to catch Deshi's eyes; he was sitting at a table with the boys from his room. I smiled at him weakly, and he waved back, but continued eating. At that moment, I understood how much we hadn't learned to give to each other at that terrible place, far from our parents, without their warmth and love. We only had what we had managed to get from home in the village. The memories began to disappear within the new reality of our lives, and also we had grown up and disappeared into the "re-education" program. I already had tired of expecting my mother, though her picture remained in my head.

Everyone got on the trucks, and I remained seated. The principal came to me and asked "Are you recovering?" I looked down and answered, "Yes, miss, I'm getting better."

She sat down next to me, and I started to tremble because I knew that the time had come---I had to tell the story I had made up. I started to speak in a weak but stable voice: "I went to the truck, apparently I was last, but I'm not sure... I felt something covering my face, and before I managed to scream, they covered my mouth. I felt they were dragging me and putting me into one of the sheds. I didn't see who it was, I only heard two men speaking." I asked for a little water because I had to calm my rapidly beating heart, and then I continued: "I heard them talking among themselves, and understood that someone had sent them. They called him Kuan and said that he had asked for a girl, but that I seemed a little too old. They said they would leave me outside the shed and go back to him to ask whether to bring me."

The principal glared into my eyes, and I felt as if she was entering my head through them in order to find out the truth.

"And they came back?" she asked.

"No," I said. "I stayed until the morning, and when I heard the men who work with us in the fields, I was still afraid to come out. Only when the children came did I run out toward them."

The principal got up from her place, grabbed me by the shirt, and pulled me up onto my feet. "All of a sudden you ran?" she asked in a rage. "And what about the covering, it disappeared just like that?"

I started crying and began to whimper. "If you don't believe me, then punish me," I cried out through the tears. "It's really too bad that they didn't kidnap me to another place, because there's no place worse than this!" I yelled loudly, and despite my unstable trembling legs, I tried to stand up straight.

"You will definitely receive a punishment you've never dreamed of," said the principal though her teeth, and then she seized my arm and dragged me to the little room at the end of the corridor. She threw me inside, and I fell on the cold floor as if my body was weightless, I fell into the darkness as she slammed and locked the door.

***

What happened during the following days I never told to anyone, because who would have believed that a young girl like me would last for entire days with no food or water, would be beaten every hour only because she had lied, only because she had wanted to get her life back, only because she had played at night with friends, only because she had wanted to return to her mother.

At first, I would ask for forgiveness and cry every time that the principal came in with the whip in her hand. I pleaded as I never had before, and made all the promises I could. I said nothing about my being an only daughter, because I already knew that that would only annoy her more. Later on, I stopped crying, and after that I stopped screaming, and the darkness penetrated me.

In between the principal's frequent visits throughout the day, I tried to fall asleep on the cold floor. The coolness was pleasant against the bloody welts scratches. I tried not to think about anything. I woke up only when the door opened. Even when the principal yelled to get up—I didn't get up. I lay with my face toward the floor, in an attempt to protect it from the whip. I felt the principal's small but strong foot kick my ribs, and sometimes she managed to pick me up when she pulled me, but mostly she whipped hard at my legs, buttocks, back, and head, and only then did she leave. Only when I heard the door slam again did I turn around to try to lean on my wounded back—with no success.

Time stood still, and the beatings only increased in intensity. I heard the lashes – the whistling of the dense air in the room when the principal heaved the leather strap. The high-pitched sound the whip made when it landed on my bare back, that's all I heard. I already could not feel the blows, or the pain. I didn't know whether it was morning or night, I no longer cared; I only wanted to stop hearing.

The wastes my body produced bothered me for the first few days; the smell was awful, and nauseated me with every breath. Each moment that passed turned the smell of my feces into a part of me, it returned to my body, filled it with the stench. Eventually, I no longer smelled it, didn't see it, I was neither hungry nor thirsty; I only heard and prayed that the sound would also disappear, and with it my thoughts, and I would die.

***

There's no way of knowing how much time passed before they returned me to my room. Maybe a week, or maybe more. I entered the room with weak knees, and could only hear Seyoung cry when she saw me. She helped me lie down, and brought me water. I didn't manage to open my eyes, and, obviously, I could not speak. I lay in my room on the mattress, numb. Seyoung gave me a drink in the morning, and tried to feed me in the evening, when she came back from working in the field. Many days passed before I managed to walk without assistance, and only then did I start eating in the large hall with everyone again.

On one of the days, the assistant principal came up to me and said: "You will no longer be going out to the fields. From now on, you will stay in the house, and clean up after everyone." I did not care anymore; I had surrendered. For a moment, my body dropped as if I had been whipped again on my lower back. I tried hard not to cry, but the tears fell of their own accord. Fear had not only silenced the words, but had paralyzed what was inside of me.

Aside from the fact that I was forbidden to go out, and could not breathe the outside air, I was happy to be doing the work in the home, which was much less difficult than the work in the fields. I cleaned every corner of the children's home. First, I cleaned the bathrooms adjacent to the principal's and her assistant's rooms, which were used only by them. They weren't so dirty, certainly not compared to what was in our bathing area. Afterwards, I cleaned their rooms. I tried not to miss a single speck of dust.

Only when I had finished cleaning the rooms, did I begin the large hall where we assembled and ate. I did not rest for a second, but the pace of my work there did not tire me like that in the fields. Though there were times when I raised my head to find the rays of the sun, I still preferred cleaning inside the children's home to working in the rice fields. Years later, when I would work as a cleaner, I would be thorough and good, and my boss would value me greatly. In the children's home, I just took the fact that they did not shout at me as a sign that I had cleaned well.

One evening, when we had gone to the hall where we ate, Ms. Ushi-He was waiting for us, with another woman beside her whom we had never seen before. I hoped that she would replace the assistant principal.

"Everyone, say hello to Ms. Shuang," said Ms. Ushi-He.

"Hello, Ms. Shuang," we answered in unison, and Ms. Shuang smiled at us.

For the first time in years, someone had smiled at us. "Ms. Shuang was sent to us by the government to teach you how to read and write," Ms. Ushi-He announced dramatically. "The government would like you to make your contributions also in clerical work, not only out in the fields. From tomorrow, you will have classes twice a week instead of working, and whoever excels in their studies will receive additional study hours."

Ms. Shuang continued to smile, and because of her smile, I wanted to believe that something good could actually happen to me. I remembered that my mother had wanted me to learn to read and write, and not be like her, and therefore, that same night, I lay down on my back and spoke with her: "Mother, I am going to learn to read and write. When I return to the village, you will be proud of me."

Seyoung nudged me with her elbow and said sleepily, "Enough, Ming, speak quietly. We want to sleep." I smiled at her, and fell asleep with that smile on my face, though I did not know yet that this time, fate would not disappoint me.

The Central Kingdom

The coming days were days that I wanted to remember every time I thought of my years at the children's home. On the days we studied, most of the children were happy for the rest we got from the work in the fields, but I looked forward to the classes to learn, and not to rest.

I eagerly swallowed everything Ms. Shuang told us about reading and writing. Ms. Shuang drew a new word in Chinese on our new board, asked us to look closely at how it was written, and then we needed to photograph it and store it in our memory. That's how we learned to read and write words. The first word we learned was "China," which was written with two characters meaning "the central kingdom." At that time, I didn't know what I would know soon after that – that there were other countries in the world, and that China was not the central country—but I will always remember how excited I was that day by the look of the first characters that I learned to read, and from the way my country was represented as the center of the world.

In one day of study, we could learn several words that are characters, and later we put sentences together with Ms. Shuang. I also reviewed and practiced what we learned on days when everyone went out to the fields and I stayed to straighten things up. As time went on, my strong desire to learn and my diligence in preparing the homework, earned me special treatment from Ms. Shuang. One morning, after everyone had gone out and I was cleaning the hall where we ate (which by that time was also used for learning reading and writing), Ms. Shuang approached me and asked why I did not go out with the others to the fields.

"I am a firstborn," I told her, tired of trying to convince people who didn't believe me. "I was taken by mistake with the children of the night because I was playing with them the night the police came to the village." I stopped when I felt the lump in my throat.

"So why are you here?" asked Ms. Shuang.

"My mother hasn't come to take me home, and I have no idea why she hasn't come," I said, all choked up. "Since then, I have been here, and with all the years that have passed, I doubt she'll ever come. I used to go out with everyone to work in the fields, but I was kidnapped, and the principal thought that I tried to escape, and that's why they don't let me out anymore."

I was quiet for a minute, and then I added, trying to swallow the lump in my throat, "I am happy that you came to teach us, I am happy to learn how to read and write."

Ms. Shuang gave me a little smile. I didn't know how much she believed me, but at least she didn't push me onto the floor or scream at me. From that moment, I loved her.

***

Time passed and I poured myself into my language studies. For the first time since I had been taken from my home, I felt that there was something filling up my life. It was fun to get up for another day of studies, and the only thoughts that took over my head that I couldn't push aside were the memories from the punishment room. The hunger from those days didn't disturb me more than the feeling that maybe I wouldn't make it, but the whipping that I had received from the assistant principal during the course of the day left scars on my body, and even deeper scars on my soul. When Ms. Shuang would ask me why I was so pensive, I answered that I was thinking of the new words.

One morning, I approached Ms. Shuang, who received me as always with a greeting and a smile. "I can already write long sentences, so I thought to write a letter to my parents," I told her proudly. "Would you please be able to send it for me?" I asked.

Ms. Shuang stopped smiling. The look she gave me caused me to shrink away, and I didn't manage to look in her eyes. "Bring it to me," she whispered quietly in my ear, "and make sure that no one ever finds out about it, no one at all." My heart was beating so hard, it seemed like I was listening to it from the outside. I decided to write to my parents in hiding, and make sure that Seyoung didn't see it, and so I waited for everyone to fall asleep, and only after I was sure that Seyoung was asleep did I start to write.

The first letter of my life I wrote over three nights, for fear that I would get caught. Now when I write books, I still write at night—which remains the most productive time for me. I decided not to say in the letter what was really happening to me. I only wanted them to come and get me, and I would tell them all the rest after I got back to the village. I wrote a very short letter because it was important to me not to make mistakes, and I was glad that whoever would read it would certainly tell my parents that I was an exemplary writer.

This is what I wrote: My mother and father, I am still waiting at the children's home in Artung for you to come and take me. I am learning to read and write, and hope that someone is reading this letter to you, so that you'll know where I am and come to get me. I have friends here and a teacher. There is a principal and assistant principal. Your daughter, Ming.

On a separate piece of paper, I wrote the names of my parents and the name of the village. I didn't know what else to write. I hugged the letter the entire night after I wrote it, and my dreams were about my return to the village. After three sleepless nights, I looked for Ms. Shuang for the one moment where I would be sure that neither the principal nor her assistant would be around. It was hard to find such a moment, and I was afraid to miss the opportunity that had been given to me. A few more days passed, and the letter was still hidden between my pants and my stomach, which was grumbling in fear, lest I be caught.

A week after I had finished writing the later, Ms. Shuang approached me at breakfast. "I received a reading book for beginners, and would like you to try to read it," she said, and passed me the book. "When you finish, return it to me, and put in it your heart's desire," she added with a smile.

The day just dragged on. I cleaned all the dishes, and especially made sure that nobody would get angry with me that day. I washed the floor on my hands and knees, and scrubbed the stones as if they were parts of my own body. I cleaned the drinking and bathing faucets, which had never been so shiny. I even cleaned the bathroom pits without being repulsed. I cleaned and cleaned, looking forward to the night, to the book waiting for me, and to my letter.

In the evening, I ate quickly and immediately got up to start cleaning. When I finished cleaning up after everyone, I went into our room. I lay down next to Seyoung, took the book in my hands and asked her, "Would you like me to read to you out loud?" Seyoung, who wasn't an especially diligent student, looked at the book and with a tired voice said, "Yes, I very much want you to, but when I fall asleep, read quietly."

With trembling hands, I opened the first book I ever read in my life. Aware of the great excitement of this occasion, I swallowed my saliva and started to read. This was a story about a group of white swans, and another swan who had been born with black feathers. To my surprise, Seyoung did not fall asleep, and asked me not to stop reading. Other friends from the room came over to us, sat near us, and listened. I looked at the children around me, who listened to me wide-eyed, and was glad that I was the one who was providing them with these magical moments.

When I finished reading, I put the book next to my mattress, and waited for everyone to return to their mattresses and fall asleep. When I heard the deep breaths of all my roommates, I put the letter folded in half into the middle of the book, lay down on the mattress, and fell asleep hugging the book close to my chest.

***

The next day at breakfast, I returned the book to Ms. Shuang. "I read the book to all the children in the room, and they all really enjoyed it," I told her excitedly. "Could you bring us more books?" I asked. Ms. Shuang gave me a satisfied smile, and said, "Of course. I'll ask them to send me other books for you." I knew in my heart that the letter was delivered. I would be forever grateful to Ms. Shuang for that.

I never spoke about the letter again, and I tried not to think about it constantly, but my imagination did not stop with the letter that was sent. Almost every night, I imagined my parents receiving the letter, going with it to the assembly hall in the village, and looking for someone who could read it to them. I saw them overcome by the words and crying, packing a small bag and taking the document from the hospital; I saw them at the door of the children's home.

I tried to focus on my cleaning so that no one would complain, and so I could continue learning with Ms. Shuang. And so it was, until one evening when the principal and her assistant were standing outside, near the gate, waiting for everyone to return from the fields. This unusual event aroused my suspicion, and it was clear to me that something had happened. Everyone got off the trucks, and the last one was Deshi, bent over, and wet from head to toe. The assistant principal walked toward him, and even though he was more than two heads taller, she grabbed him by the collar and dragged him, the submissive, to the punishment room. I ran to look for Ms. Shuang, and I thought that if I told her what had happened to me in there, maybe she would help free Deshi; but unfortunately, I didn't find her. I asked his friends what had happened, and they said that he had tried to escape, but had been caught by the men. I ran to the punishment room and banged on the door.

"Take me instead," I begged. "Leave him alone, please! He didn't mean to run away." The door opened and the principal pushed me away from the door. "If you don't stop right now, you will be punished too," she said fiercely. At the sound of her words, my body felt every scar all over again. I knew that my body was more fragile than that of Deshi, but despite his physical strength, I was afraid he wouldn't be able to withstand the terrible hunger, and that the daily whippings would break his spirit. I collapsed on the floor near the door to the little room and prayed that he would make it through.

When the principal and her assistant came out of there, they screamed at me to continue cleaning, otherwise they would immediately punish me too. I went back to cleaning, and the cleaning water mixed with the tears that flowed endlessly from my eyes. At night, I couldn't fall asleep. The scars hurt me, I couldn't stop thinking of Deshi, and I couldn't fall asleep. Seyoung, who tried to calm me, asked that I tell her the story of the ducks again, but I couldn't even answer her; I never told even her exactly what had happened to me in that room, even though she saw me when I came out of there.

***

The next day after breakfast, everyone went out for another day's work. I heard the trucks driving away, and at the same time, I heard the engine of another vehicle that stayed outside the children's home. The principal screamed that I return to our room, and that I not leave it until she called me. I stood close to the door of the room, and could hear at least two men speaking with the principal. I put my ear on the door, but couldn't understand what they were talking about. I thought maybe an inspector had arrived, and after he had seen Deshi, would immediately end the punishment. I wanted to think that maybe a doctor had arrived because Deshi did not feel well.

I heard the men passing in the corridor, and after a while

I didn't hear them any longer, and understood that they had left. When I heard the car ignition, I went out of the room. The corridor was empty. I went to the punishment room and saw that the door was open. I peeked inside—Deshi was not there. I ran outside. The two women stood in the doorway and watched the car drive off. "Where is Deshi?" I yelled at them.

"Go back inside right now, and don't you dare raise your voice again!" screamed the principal. They never told us what had happened to him, and I could only guess that he had not withstood the whippings and humiliation. I could also only guess that they hadn't taken him to a doctor or an inspector. That night, I cried myself to sleep. That was the night that I stopped dreaming of my parents, and stopped believing that they would come and take me home. That night, I understood that fate had taken me from the village, but that same fate would not return me there.

Instead of burying myself in thoughts of Deshi, my fate, and that of all my friends there, I tried to delve into my cleaning work and reading. I found that if I thoroughly cleaned the rooms of the principal and her assistant, they would let me read and practice writing while the others were working in the fields. I found that that was a new way to escape. I escaped to places when I started to read about them. In my imagination, I traveled to the places that I read about in books, smelled them, and heard what happened in them, and I could enjoy my cleaning work that enabled me to wander to places that I "had already been to" though I would never, or so I believed, actually get to them.

Lin

I read books that taught me about the world beyond the mountains that encircled my village; a world that I doubted existed as I read in the children's home. There were days that I read to my friends from the books I had, and there were books that I read to myself in bed, sometimes all night. I hoped for the day when I would have children, and I would be able to read books to them. I dreamed of many children, not just one, children who would stay with me all their lives, who could sleep at night, and enjoy life during the day.

In the meantime, I read in the children's home, to myself and to the other children, and out of all the books I read, there was one book that I loved more than any other. The hero of this story was Lin, a young girl from New York who introduced me to the big city. Years later, when I got to a big city, I thought it was Lin's New York. When I read the description of the girl, I had the feeling that she looked like me: she had Chinese eyes, prominent cheekbones, and smooth black hair—all of these reminded me of myself. For several nights, I lived her life. I couldn't put the book down. I loved the girl's character, identified with her aspirations, but more than anything, I was interested in her relationship with her mother. The whole time I read the book I had a strong longing for my mother, and couldn't stop thinking about the relationship that would have developed between us if I hadn't been taken from her. On one of the days, I read the following passage:

Lin decided to forgive her mother when the curtain went down. The lights came on all at once and illuminated the stage on which all the actors were already standing, holding hands and smiling at the audience that was loudly applauding. After a few minutes, the spectators got up and continued to clap at a steady rhythm that filled the hall with powerful sounds, echoing off the high ceiling.

The theater was a luxurious hall from the 1920s that had recently been refurbished as part of the renovations that were being carried out in Broadway performance halls. The ceiling was very colorful, as if whoever had painted the wood in the Gothic style had deliberately exaggerated the colors. The walls were more like those of a Catholic church supported by tall pillars, and there was little ornamentation. The color of the walls was quiet, and did not attract any special attention. The chairs were on one level, and the stage was higher, unlike halls where the floor slopes up and the audience looks down on the stage from above.

I felt I was sitting next to Lin, applauding along with her. When I read the book, I didn't even know what shows were, and I certainly couldn't imagine the fancy theaters as Lin had described them. But her detailed description of the hall caused me to imagine that I was sitting next to her. Like her, I wanted to forgive my mother.

One by one, the actors came forward and bowed to the audience, and each one received loud cheers that died down by the time the next actor started walking forward. Last but not least, Yan-Tao came to the front of the stage. He was the

Chinese lead actor who displayed very convincing acting ability despite the fact that he wasn't American.

Lin clapped loudly until her hands hurt. She felt an irritation in her throat, and the tears flowed down her cheeks before she could wipe them with the tissue she had prepared. Lin in the book already knew why she cried, and why she forgave, and her crying was cathartic. I, who was still at the children's home, still didn't know why I would cry, and certainly I still didn't know that I would not feel any relief from the pain.

Lin didn't read reviews of plays before she watched them, and always preferred to go to shows without any advance knowledge. That time she decided to read... after all, Jillian, her friend from work, had strongly recommended the play, told her about the story in great detail, and described the goose bumps she felt watching the Chinese actor Yan-Tao at work.

This was his first Broadway play, despite his advanced age. The reviews praised the show, and everyone asked the obvious question: why did it take so many years for Yan-Tao to finally act on stage in New York? In London, he often appeared in plays and large productions, and reaped praise for his acting ability, and for his unaccented English. "He studied theater in New York, and returned to his birthplace at the end of his studies," Jillian ended her lecture.

Lin bought a ticket for the play, though she never went to a show alone, because she didn't want to feel awkward. For Lin, a play was something you went to with friends, like going to a restaurant or a pub, or anywhere else. I read these words and didn't understand them. I had no idea what restaurants or pubs were.

When I read the book, I felt as if I was sitting close to Lin, and I also saw the play as Lin had described it: I saw the actors, marveled at the scenery, the costumes, and the lights. I wanted to hold her hand, but I couldn't. She was sitting alone, and so was I.

Lin received the love of theater from her mother, who went with her to most of the shows she saw. The conversations between them fascinated me. I read again and again every-thing that Lin's mother had said to her. I wanted my mother to also talk to me, guide me, tell me, teach me. She never got angry with her, and always wanted her to join her. She nev-er left her with a babysitter, and always took her with her to friends, museums, and of course to plays. And I also so want-ed a friend-mother, and I wouldn't need plays or museums—I just wanted to go back home. I longed for my mother's scent, for the foods she prepared, the songs she sang me, and the smile on her face every time she saw me. When Lin was 14 years old, she said that she would be an actress when she grew up, and her mother only smiled in response and said nothing. But when Lin grew up, her mother refused to let her do that. "Learn any profession," she told her, "just not theater." Lin's mother was silent for a moment and later she added, "There's no need at all to study theater."

When I read these lines, I was about 16 years old, and I still had no idea what I would do when I grew up.

Lin's mother didn't take her daughter's desire to be an ac-tress seriously. All of Lin's attempts to convince her, including mentioning the fact that her mother had studied theater her-self and had not become an actress, didn't make a difference.

If I could have discussed the course of my life with my mother, if she had come to take me from that place, maybe we would have found differences of opinion between us. I couldn't remember any argument I had had with my mother, but I wanted her to be with me when I got older, to guide, advise, assist. I wanted to remember something of my relationship with my mother, for a moment I even got angry that she had given up on me. I also thought about my father, and I was amazed that Lin had not asked about her father. As if it's considered normal there, in New York, for there to be only one parent.

In Lin's mother's photo album, there were slightly yellowed pictures of the shows she had been in as an acting student. Lin loved to sit on the couch and look through the albums over and over. In the albums there were pictures of her mother dressed in rags in the play "Les Miserables," and of her as a housewife, and in one she has long hair and colorful beads as a hippy in "Hair". I read the names of these plays and immediately wrote them in the notebooks I had received in the children's home. I pictured myself watching these shows one day.

Since she knew that she wouldn't be able to make her mother change her mind regarding acting studies, like she couldn't divert Earth from its course, when she finished high school, Lin decided to register for law school at the prestigious Columbia University in New York. During the years of her studies, Lin would help her mother at the bookstore. The work in the store helped her relieve some of the stress of the studies, and her mother was happy that her daughter was with her in the store they both loved. They continued to go to plays together, but they no longer spoke about acting studies.

After Lin finished her internship at one of the large law firms in the city, she was comforted by her successful court appearances. When the judge entered the court, Lin imagined the curtain going up, and that she was starring in the role of the lawyer. Her clients always praised her for her court appearances, and she felt that she put her soul into their cases. The court was her stage, and she would invite her mother to see her appear. "Don't forget that you mustn't clap at the end," she would remind her every time, but that didn't stop her mother from getting up to applaud her daughter, until the security people were forced to remove her from the courtroom. Lin so loved her mother that she never got angry at her behavior in court; it just amused her.

But this happiness did not last very long since Lin's mother became ill. For a long time, she hid her serious illness from Lin, and only when she was forced to close the store for her constant treatments did she tell her daughter about it. Lin took it hard, but after she got over the most intense pain, she offered to quit her work so she could help her mother. Obviously, Lin's mother flatly refused to have her daughter stay with her all day, and I thought to myself that my mother wouldn't have agreed for me to take care of her either. The thought of my mother hurt me so much that I didn't want to think about that anymore.

The day before Lin's mother died, Lin lost a case that had been very important to her, and she felt terrible because of it. She hurried to the hospital as if hypnotized, as she knew the route very well. Her mother saw her bad mood, and with the last of her strength, she managed to ask her what the matter was.

"I didn't manage to defend my client," Lin said, her voice breaking, "and I feel that that's not right."

"Don't be angry, my Lin," her mother said slowly and quietly. "Try not to be angry, not at others, and not at me," she added weakly.

That same night, she told Lin what she had never dared

speak about. And that same night, I didn't manage to fall asleep. How many secrets do people have, I thought to myself, how is it possible to hide such a secret? It even came into my head that maybe my mother had a secret, and maybe I am not really her firstborn daughter, and that was why she hadn't managed to return me to bring me back to her. All night I tossed and turned, until Seyoung got angry that I had woken her up.

***

Lin left the hospital and ran to her mother's house. She picked up a photo album in her trembling hands, and paged through the pictures. She prepared a cup of tea for herself, and tried not to cry, not over her mother and her illness, not for herself, not over her future without her mother, and not over what she'd told her.

Since she did not find what she was looking for in the albums, she sat and stared into space until her eyes focused on her mother's giant bookcase. She remembered that her mother had a yearbook that she had kept because she always said that it contained the prettiest picture of her, a picture where she looked happy. Lin went straight to the bookcase, took out the yearbook, and started looking for that picture. She so wanted to see her mother happy, she hadn't seen her that way for a long time, and she had even forgotten her smile. When she continued going through the yearbook, and saw the pictures of her mother's school friends, she understood, and didn't know whether to be angry or happy.

The next day, after a sleepless night, she went to the hospital, with many questions she wanted to ask her mother.

Mainly she wanted to ask her why she had only now told her the secret. She found her mother lying down with her eyes closed, with a respirator and a morphine drip. She didn't open her eyes, not even when she heard Lin's voice telling her what had happened to her since she had left the day before. Only later did Lin's mother open her eyes for a second, take a last look at her daughter, gather all her energy for a last farewell smile, and close her eyes forever.

A sharp knife sliced Lin's chest and continued on to mine. She felt the pain of loss, pain which I had fought all those years not to feel. I still clung to the hope that even after so many years, my mother would ultimately come. In my imagination, I was again standing with Lin, and I tried to hold her hand, but she remained alone. The ground moved under her feet, and she tried to prevent herself from falling, to convince herself that her mother had been redeemed from terrible suffering that had lasted many months. But the logic didn't help. The ground continued to move and larger and larger cracks appeared underneath her, and any minute, Lin would fall and disappear into one of the cracks. Pits opened around her, and she tried to grab something, so as not to fall, her body was weightless and likely to be torn from the ground. Reading those words, I understood that I had not yet felt a real sense of loss; I understood that I was holding on tightly to hope and memory, and that I was still standing on firm ground. I was afraid to feel like an orphan.

Only for one thing did Lin not forgive her mother until the curtain came down, that only just before her death did she tell her for the first time that her father had also been an acting student and had become a famous and beloved actor.

Lin's story never left my head. I pictured her in the big city of New York, I saw her walking around with her mother, going with her everywhere, and I felt how she had forgiven her for everything. And I too wanted to forgive.

A Hairy Mole

One morning, Ms. Shuang called me and told me to go in to the principal. In the short hallway that led to her room, I already had bad thoughts in my head. I remembered how I had run to the assistant principal's room when Anchi died. I could feel again the stomachache that I got when I saw her curled-up body. The sight of the slight corpse wrapped in a little sheet stayed with me for a long time. Today I am 19 years old, and I still often wake up drenched in sweat from a dream in which I was wrapped in a little sheet, like the sheet that was wrapped around Anchi.

In that moment, I deeply missed Anchi and her brother. I wanted to hug her again as I had on the truck that brought us to the children's home. I felt deep pain that I hadn't kept my promise to help her, to protect her. I was afraid they would tell me to go back to working in the fields, and that upset me very much. The possibility of learning and reading raised my spirits very much, and because of that, I enjoyed my days in a way I'd never thought possible after so many years at that place.

With my right hand I knocked gently on the principal's door, and with my left hand I wiped the tears that had managed to escape. I took a deep breath to try to calm myself down. "Yes, come in," the principal called. I was very much afraid, and I entered, heart pounding.

"I have a special task for you today," the principal told me in a serious voice which this time did not sound threatening. "Our driver needs to pick up things arriving from Hong Kong for the children's home. Since he doesn't know the way to the border, which is a few hours' drive from here, I need you to ride with him and read the road signs to him."

My eyes filled with tears, but in contrast to the tears that I had cried until that day, this time they were tears of happiness. Since I had never before experienced such tears, I was surprised that they too were salty, and flowed uncontrollably onto my cheeks. Mixed into their saltiness, apparently, were smiles and giggles that I barely managed to suppress.

"Ms. Shuang told me that I can rely on you," the principal added. "She said that you'll know how to read everything, and you'll be able to help the driver during the trip." My whole body was smiling and happy at the sound of these words. A short time later, when I got into the truck, all my friends looked at me, and I smiled and waved at everyone. In the truck I recognized the driver by the large mole on his face, out of which grew long black hairs. It was the driver that I had seen during the first days at the children's home, the driver that I had told then, as I told everyone that I saw along the way, that I was a firstborn. I also begged him to tell my mother where I was. I remember that I had managed to tell him that I was a firstborn, but the assistant principal quickly and angrily brought me inside, and he didn't get to hear who I was and where I was from. I wasn't angry that he hadn't tried to help, because he, like myself, had also apparently received orders from above, or as part of the re-education, he had learned to keep his mouth shut

The mole on his face reminded me of a few of the men from my village. They never plucked out the long hairs from their moles, so they always seemed strange to me. I remember that there were superstitions regarding the hairs growing from moles on men's faces, but I didn't remember exactly what they were. At that time, when I sat in the truck next to the driver with the mole, I only wanted to believe that they were a sign of nice people.

***

The ride was extremely bumpy. The driver didn't talk to me and didn't ask me anything. I told him that when he wanted me to read a particular sign for him, that he should point to it. He nodded in response. After a fairly long segment of the ride, he stopped and got out of the truck. Since he hadn't said anything to me, I remained frozen in my place. I didn't even know what I should be afraid of. I felt so happy to go out on this ride, and I didn't want to ruin the feeling for myself. I very much wanted to see what was on the other side of the mountains. I hoped that maybe I would also see places from the books that I had read. The only rides I had ever taken were to the children's home at night, and to the rice fields each and every day until I was punished, and I was happy that I had been prohibited from going out to them. This ride was different; it was my first happy moment in years. I already knew that there was a whole other world outside, and I wanted to see it. I remembered Dewei-Hu's stories, the artist that made wagons for the people in the villages beyond the mountains, about life in those villages. I remembered the wagon that he had made for us, the pockets my mother had attached to the seats, the happiness we knew in our daily routine.

A few minutes later the driver with the hairy mole returned. After he tied his pants, he continued driving. As time passed, he quietly pointed at more and more signs, and I read them for him. On every sign were names of cities or places that I had never heard of. The number that appeared after the name Hong Kong became lower and lower, and that's how I understood that we were approaching our destination. It made sense that the number on the sign was getting lower and lower, but each kilometer that passed made me sad. I wanted the ride to continue on and on, for more days, and even more weeks.

This drive did not have complicated instructions or cleaning, only the sound of the motor running. When I opened the window, the wind blew pleasantly on my face. I looked at the flat view around, and I didn't find the magic I thought I would see when I traveled far away. Sometimes I saw rice fields that looked very much like the ones we worked at, and when we got close to cities whose names were on a sign, we also saw roads full of cars. Later we also traveled on empty roads, and everything was new, interesting, and intriguing.

When we got close to cities, we saw lots of people, a sight that was new to me but I knew about it from books I had read. I remembered in Ms. Shuang's class when she told us how big China was, and at the same time, I couldn't understand what she meant. Ms. Shuang spoke proudly about our country and our leader. She told us a lot about the government and what it did, but during that time, all I could do was long for my mother. Apparently, I managed to understand what the size of the Central Kingdom was, I remembered that there were cities crowded with people, but all this didn't prepare me for what I saw later.

When we arrived at the border station in Shenzhen, as was written on the large sign when we reached the city, we were asked to get off the truck. The driver presented the documents to a guard standing at the entrance to a long one-story building, and, in response, the guard pointed to another door, and we went into a little hall. "We must wait here," the driver said tersely," the first words he'd said to me the entire day.

In the hall there were two rows of attached seats, and hanging on the wall, next to the Chinese flag, was a picture of the leader. In about an hour, they called the driver. "I am going out to load the goods," he said. That was the second sentence that he said to me that day, and I noticed that his voice was pleasant and not aggressive. I smiled and thought to myself that apparently the hairs of the mole were indeed a sign of nice people. A few moments after he left, I saw a sign indicating the bathroom, and I went there. To this very day, I smile at the shock I got at the sight of the Western bathrooms. For the first time in my life I saw a chair with a hole in the middle. It took time until I understood how to use it. After years knowing only about toilets with a hole in the floor, sitting on the seat was clumsy but exciting.

I returned to the waiting area, and sat at the end of a row of seats. I sat smiling, excited from the travel experience, from the people that I saw, and of course from the new toilets. Many people were entering and exiting the waiting room, but no one looked at me and asked what I was doing there.

***

After a while, I had already memorized every mark on the

walls of the waiting room. My stomach grumbled and hurt from hunger. I fell asleep sitting in a chair, and when I woke up in panic, I had no idea how many hours or even days I had been waiting there for the driver, who had not come back to take me. The sun had already set, and the waiting room sank into gloom. Fate, I thought to myself, was playing with my life as if I had no needs or feelings.

Finally, I got up and went toward the door. It was dark outside, the sun had disappeared, and with it all the people who had been there. I didn't see any cars or trucks, there was no guard by the second door of the building, I didn't see anyone, and I didn't know whether to be happy about that or not. I only knew that the driver with the hairy mole had disappeared.

I left the hall and started to run. There was no one around; night had taken over the deserted place. I didn't know which way to run, but I felt that despite my hunger and weak muscles, I would be able to run fast for a long time. I had run away again, but this time without planning. I had already heard the sound of my heavy breaths running with me, and for a moment I stopped and looked at the stars, maybe they would provide a clue to which direction to run. I looked for the one star that would sparkle, that would provide the clue that would take my hand. When I saw a falling star, I remembered that in our village, we would count falling stars. Among the children of the night, a competition developed: who saw the most falling stars? I never won those competitions then, because I was always busy playing games with my friends, and I didn't bother to stare at the sky. That night, when it was very dark, I looked at the sky to find answers, and the falling star that I saw for a fleeting moment gave me the direction to my fate.

***

The run turned into a blind march. I marched until car lights flashed at me. Hunger and fatigue did not allow me to flee from the lights, and ultimately, I fell on the ground. A car stopped next to me, and two young guys who looked older than me got out. "What happened to you?" they asked. I was afraid to answer, and actually, I had no answer. I slowly got up and looked down. Out of the corner of my eye, I could see that they were also frightened. "Are you also running away to Hong Kong?" one of them asked.

I wanted to believe that I was in control of my fate, so I said that I was. "Come with us," the guy said. "I don't think you'll be able to continue alone."

He opened the door of the car and motioned for me to sit next to the driver. I got in, trembling all over. "Welcome," I heard a whisper from the backseat. I turned my head and saw four more boys squeezed into the backseat. I couldn't see their faces clearly because of the darkness, or maybe because I was so tired.

"I don't have to sit in the front," I said when I understood that one of them had gotten into the back because of me.

"No way! We're fine," one of the boys said, "let's go, Shaohan, drive!" he said to the driver, who stepped on the gas.

They had a map drawn on paper, but I was afraid to ask questions. I didn't know what they were planning to do, I only knew that they were fleeing to Hong Kong. I knew for sure that if I told people at the children's home that I was kidnapped, no one would believe me. The ride was very slow and quiet. Every once in a while one of the boys would give instructions to the driver.

Suddenly I felt terrible nausea that went from my stomach up to my throat. I remembered that I hadn't eaten for an entire day, and I didn't know what I would manage to vomit. I remembered my ride to the children's home, and because of that memory, I opened the door as we drove and stuck my head out to throw up. The driver stopped immediately, and everyone waited in silence for me to finish.

"Excuse me," I said weakly, "I haven't eaten anything all day." One of the boys passed me a canteen. I drank all the water in it, without considering the others. When I finished drinking, I was a bit ashamed of what I had done, but I couldn't help it. The same boy gave me rice wrapped in a banana leaf, but I was too embarrassed to open the leaf after I had drunk all their water. So I just held the leaf tightly, and imagined myself eating the rice inside.

As the ride went on, I felt better, and I could follow the instructions they gave to the driver. I was comfortable in their car, even though I didn't know them. They didn't frighten me, on the contrary, I had the feeling that I was in good hands. I gave myself the freedom to continue enjoying that day. I didn't know how it would all end up, but I felt happy that I could enjoy myself, even if for a short time.

"We need to drive faster, so we get there before the sun comes up," the boy behind me said. Shaohan the driver looked at me every once in a while, and asked if everything was okay. I just said "yes" quickly, which I hoped would convince him, and the conversation didn't develop. We rode in silence as if someone would hear us.

***

As the time passed, and the ride went on, I could feel the pressure they were under from the pace of the fragmented speech of the boy giving the instructions. Shaohan the driver listened to the instructions of the boy in the back, who followed the outline of the map and drove accordingly.

"It looks like we are really close," announced the boy, and Shaohan drove faster.

All we saw was just darkness, and the lights of the little car we drove in lit up only a few meters ahead. "I think we passed the border," said Shaohan excitedly. "Jo said that we wouldn't know exactly where the border was because there's no fence, and we would just find ourselves in Hong Kong," he added.

"Until we're sure that we are there, we'll continue driving according to the map," the boy said from the back. "I have my compass out the whole time, so that we don't go wrong and return to the village," he added. I longed to ask what village they were from—maybe they had heard that I'd been taken from my mother unjustly? But I still didn't feel confident enough to reveal anything about myself.

As the time passed, I felt clearly the stress and excitement of the boys in the group. Every once in a while, Shaohan would ask if I was sure that everything was all right, and I would smile at him silently. The meaning of the name Shaohan is generous laughter, and I thought that his name fit his personality well because he was nice and generous to me. We continued driving, using the compass only. I knew what a compass was because it had been discussed somewhere in the books I'd read, but I had never seen one. In most of the stories, a compass was used as a guide, but there were stories in which the compass was used as a spiritual guide, and presented in an expression that I especially liked, "a human compass." Usually, the expression was used for someone who needed to make a decision, one way or another—someone looking for an answer which way to choose for himself, and what decision to make. Every one of us has a compass in his head, and it is what helps us decide what to choose. Each time one of the boys picked up the compass to check that we were traveling in the right direction, I wanted to believe that he was leading me to a new life, to a life that would enable me to return to my village and see my mother and father again.

The compass was leading us on a long ride until the sky was clear and the light poked through the heavy fog. I didn't see sun, only a blinding light that lit up the entire sky. Shaohan suggested we stop for the day, find a place to hide the car, and try to sleep a bit. Everyone agreed with him immediately. I could look at him now that the light allowed me to see clearly. His skin was much darker than mine. I saw his face from the side, and when he noticed that I was staring at him, he turned to smile at me. His eyes sparkled mischievously, but his smile was pleasant. Later I noticed that his ears were huge, and peeked out from under his straight hair.

I wasn't sure that I would manage to fall asleep given all the excitement and twists my life was taking. A loud squeal woke me from my thoughts, and Shaohan's yell woke up the others: "Look at these giant buildings!" He pointed at the block of buildings that seemed to me like a picture I had imagined in a book I had read. He stopped the car at the corner, and we all got out.

"We're here!" the boys yelled in chorus, and only then did I dare ask, "Where?"

"In Hong Kong!" yelled Shaohan. "Didn't you say that you were running away to Hong Kong too?"

"Yes, of course," I answered sheepishly. "I just can't believe we've already arrived."

Everyone burst out in relieved laughter that lifted the tension, laughter that thundered when they understood I had no idea where I was.

City

I felt like I was dreaming, that maybe because of the books I had read before going to sleep, I couldn't comprehend what I was seeing. I had never before seen houses with more than one floor; I only knew of houses in my village, under which burrows had been built to hide the children of the night during the day. The sight of the tall buildings didn't even frighten me—I wasn't able to process it all. I didn't understand what I saw, and I could only try to understand what the boys I was with thought of the sights. They grabbed each other's hands, and I could see the excitement in their body language.

"Are you okay?" Shaohan asked, and all of a sudden I was overcome with emotion and started crying.

"What happened? What's wrong?" asked Shaohan and grasped my hand.

I quickly understood that it wasn't the site of the impossibly large buildings that caused me to cry, rather the simple question of a stranger asking how I was, to find out if I was really all right. It had been years since anyone had cared how I was or how I felt, besides my friend Seyoung, years that no one had asked how I was, years during which I had disappeared into the children's home. And here for the first time I was facing my freedom and was overwhelmed by the attention I received.

Gradually, Shaohan got closer to me in an effort to understand why I was crying. He wasn't holding my hand so gently, but pleasantly enough that I did not pull my hand away. "What happened?" he asked again and again, until I managed to say that I was fine and that I was crying out of excitement. Shaohan didn't let go of my hand; the tears ran down my face, but I didn't dare pull my hand away and wipe them off. I had never held hands with a boy before, and I couldn't distinguish between a fatherly hold and that of a boyfriend, but I did feel that his hold was supportive. I could have continued standing there for hours with my hand in his, as I looked off at the view that I had no way of comprehending.

I stared into space, and many questions came into my head: How had I gotten there, to that wonderful place? Was it really as amazing as it seemed from afar? How had I managed to escape without intending to? What would happen if I were caught again? This question disturbed me greatly, and I needed to work hard not to think of what had happened before. I tried to convince myself to just concentrate on the view. The thoughts spun around my head: Why did the driver with the hairy mole leave me there, in that hall? And why did the boys stop to pick me up? Who were they really, and were they on my side? I was very afraid, afraid that I had put my trust in them, and allowed them to take me, and also that I didn't know them and didn't know what their intentions really were. Though the many questions running around my head confused me greatly, one thing was clear: my fate had returned to my own hands.

I was facing freedom, but I still didn't feel free. The thoughts in my head were mixed with the feelings in my heart, and created a jumble that was simultaneously agreeable and stressful. I tried to stop thinking about Shaohan's hand holding mine, or about the storm inside of me, and understand what had happened and what I needed to do. Shaohan let go of my hand, and I wiped my face and rubbed my eyes to make sure that what I was seeing was not a mirage. I took a deep breath and tried to calm down so that I could think clearly.

The boys continued to stand and marvel at the buildings that blocked the sky, at their height and the sheer number of them. They decided to look for a place to park the car and sleep. From their discussions, I understood that they were planning first of all to find work, because they had no money.

I noticed that they didn't look alike and seemed not to be from the same family. One of them, Chong, had hair that seemed strange to me, it was brown and wavy, and didn't seem to match his black Chinese eyes.

I wanted to listen to them talk, but I didn't manage to concentrate. My thoughts moved between the sights before my eyes, the words of the group, Shaohan's hand that had been holding mine, and the flutter of butterflies circling inside my stomach. I managed to concentrate on my objective, and I asked myself how I would get to my village. I stood in place, trying to free myself of the whirlpool of thoughts in my head, and in the background I heard the voices of the boys. Suddenly a loud voice sliced into my thoughts, "To the car!" Though the boy who had yelled out was standing next to me, it seemed to me that the voice had come from the other side of the mountains. I saw that everyone had already returned to the car, and I hurried to let myself in, blushing in embarrassment. After a short time, Shaohan stopped the car behind an abandoned roofless building and said: "We'll sleep a bit and then continue. Each one will stand guard for an hour and then we'll switch."

Shaohan opened the trunk of the car and called everyone to come eat. He sounded very firm, and I was alarmed by the volume of his voice. The order that he had yelled did not match the concern he had shown for me and the millions of questions he had asked me. I wondered whether he really was generous and concerned with my welfare, and that of his friends, or did he just follow instructions and give orders? I was suspicious.

Inside open cardboard boxes were banana leaves filled with rice. In another box were ears of corn and bananas. I wondered where he had acquired the food, but didn't ask—I was too hungry.

Shaohan took out a container of water and asked that everyone freshen up and wash himself in important places. The boys started laughing in embarrassment. I already knew, unfortunately, how to wash myself using little water; in the children's home we didn't have any more than that. Now, it was important to me that my body have a nice smell. I distanced myself from the group, stood to the side, and washed my face and underarms. When I finished washing, I ran back to join the circle and finally eat.

The embarrassment and excitement quickly surrendered to deep sleep. I woke up to the sound of the boys talking among themselves. I opened my eyes and wondered whether I had been dreaming or had really woken up in a car in which I had fled from China to Hong Kong with five boys. I quickly found out that my fate wasn't playing games with me this time, and that I was indeed inside a car that was not standing still. "Nice that you woke up," said one of the boys. "You must've been very, very tired because you didn't even feel that we had started to drive. We are already inside the city." While he spoke, I carefully stretched my body and tried to get out of the sitting position I had been sleeping in. I badly needed to go to the bathroom and get cleaned up, but in the meantime, I preferred to keep quiet and wait and see what fate had in store for me.

The car drove down the crowded streets of the city. The number of people on one street was greater than the number of people I had seen my entire life. I understood that we were looking for restaurants. I knew what a restaurant was from the books I'd read but had never been in one, and had never even seen one. Shaohan stopped the car next to a building that had a bright yellow sign with red letters that read: "Our Chinese Girl." He got out of the car with Chong, and we waited for them for a fairly long time. I sat in the car and watched the figures walking in front of me and around our car from every direction. I noticed that most of the men wore fancy suits and dark glasses, which made me laugh. The boys didn't know why I had laughed, and I made myself stop laughing so as not to embarrass myself further.

Shaohan came out of the restaurant with a big smile on his face, a smile I would see a lot. "One down," he said, still smiling. "Chong stayed to work as a dishwasher, and he'll get paid well." He got in behind the wheel. "I only hope that we'll be able to pick him up at night."

For the rest of the day we stopped near dozens of restaurants with signs with names that seemed strange for restaurants, but unfortunately Shaohan and the boys did not manage to repeat the success of the first restaurant. In the evening, we returned to the "Our Chinese Girl" restaurant to pick up Chong, whose clothes were very dirty, and their strong smell was soon unmistakable inside the car.

***

We returned to the place where we had parked at night. This time it took me a long time to fall asleep, and I could hear the breathing of the boys who had fallen asleep right away. That entire night, I thought about my mother, and my hope that very soon I would return to her; I thought of Seyoung who was certainly worried about me and afraid that something bad had happened; I even thought of the principal of the children's home and her assistant, and I couldn't even imagine how they had reacted when they saw that I hadn't returned. When my thoughts wandered to Ms. Shuang, I felt a pang in my heart; she had believed in me, and I apparently turned out to be a big disappointment.

That entire night, I thought of people that I loved, and of the people that had made my life unbearable. The thoughts that hopped from person to person kept me from sleeping, and only when I started to see light on the horizon did I finally fall asleep.

On the second day, Kang found work at a small restaurant as a shopper. He was asked to cut his hair because it came down to his waist.

There were four of us left, and I was afraid to ask if they would find me work too. Every time we stopped at a restaurant, Shaohan got out with one of the boys. It was clear that Shaohan was the leader of the group, and he was the one who had to take care of everyone. Along with his leadership, I noticed that his friends were a little scared of him, and they usually agreed to any suggestion he made or with any idea he came up with. However, he did take care of everyone else's needs before he took care of himself. He would also take care of me, I thought to myself, and little did I know I would soon be proven correct.

After about five days of searching, Shaohan and I were the only ones without work. At the end of each day, we picked up everyone and rode to sleep in the usual spot. Our suppers widely varied, thanks to the food that the boys brought from the restaurants they worked at. We refilled the water containers every day to wash ourselves. The boys had extra clothes in the car, and I received some item of clothing from each of them. They were too big for me but were clean. I washed my clothes in water from the containers, and left them to dry at our night parking spot.

The boys spoke of how they would rent an apartment together as soon as they had enough money. I didn't understand what they meant, but I had decided not to ask questions. After many years my fate had turned in an interesting direction, and I decided to submit to it in the faith that this time I was on the right path.

The next morning, after we had brought everyone to the various restaurants, just Shaohan and myself remained in the car. "Now us," he said and smiled his wide smile. "I think we'll try to get work at a hotel in the city." He looked at me and waited for my response, and I understood that my silence was awkward for him, and it certainly didn't do anything for me. So I decided to ask questions, and the dam was broken. The flood of queries that I poured on him included questions regarding their plans as a group, and his finding work for himself, and finally regarding me. Shaohan was happy to reply. I already understood that they had left for Hong Kong to find a better future. He didn't go into details why they had fled, because he apparently assumed that I too was looking for a better future, and so he saw no need to elaborate. I understood that they hadn't escaped from a children's home, rather their parents had encouraged them to leave and provided them with a car and explanations. Regarding the question what would be with me, Shaohan said, "For now, you are with me." Since that answer was agreeable to me, I stopped asking questions.

We stopped near the Golden Tulip hotel, and then we went in to the Sheraton and the Hilton, and other hotels after that, for the entire day. In the evening, we picked up everyone from their work places, and decided to continue looking the next day. After many days of searching, we understood that hotels did not want to employ foreigners, and certainly not two together.

The Big Buddha

Another day went by and then another week, during which we looked for work, but to no avail. Despair first hit Shaohan and then me, only after I understood how frustrated he was at having failed to find work after so many attempts.

"Maybe you should find work for yourself alone at a restaurant?" I asked one morning, after everyone had gone off to their jobs. For a moment, Shaohan stopped smiling his usual smile, put on a serious look, and said: "I brought you here and therefore I am responsible for you. And besides that, I really like you and have no intention of letting you go so quickly."

I felt my cheeks burning and looked down. I leaned my face on one hand, and in that way hid at least one hot, red cheek. I tried to reconstruct the sentence he had said in my head to be sure that I had understood correctly. In the children's home there were couples that had gotten together, especially during the last year. But I, who was so busy reading and cleaning, felt like I was in a big house with lots of brothers and sisters. I remembered every description that I had read of butterflies. Many times in books that I read, I was excited for the heroes of the story; the butterflies left the books and flew toward me, and filled my stomach, and they did not stop to rest. Now many butterflies entered my stomach, tried to fly together in the small space, caused a commotion, bumping into each other, their wings tied to all my internal organs.

"This morning, we aren't going to look for work," announced Shaohan unexpectedly. "This morning, let's go on a trip." And he turned the car away from the bustling city. We drove quietly for a pretty long time. I wanted to ask him many questions: I wanted to know if I would stay with him forever, if his responsibility for me was limited in time, but I concentrated on the nice feelings I had, plus I felt awkward asking the questions that I wanted to. I was completely involved in analyzing Shaohan's sentence that I didn't even notice that he was fully concentrating on driving. I had no feeling of time, the sights from the car window went past me but I didn't see them. I was focused within myself, and only stole a look at Shaohan every once in a while, hoping he wouldn't notice. After a while, he asked me to read the signs and tell him when we'd reached a sign saying "The Big Buddha." I smiled happily that I was again reading signs.

But the waves that started to rise up and crash in my stomach became a storm every time he spoke to me, and this new feeling swept me away and made me so dizzy that I had a hard time concentrating on the signs and what they said. I fought the butterflies and the waves so they would move from my field of vision, and allow me to see the signs along the way. When I saw the first sign with the words "The Big Buddha" on it, I dared to ask Shaohan, "Where are we driving to?"

"The Big Buddha is a big statue," he said, "and whoever was at this place told me that it is one of the most beautiful sights there is. I thought that after I'd found work we would all drive there, but this morning I decided that I wanted to see it with you. The job hunt can wait another day for us, because I need a little quiet." I had been slowly gathering my moments of happiness, and my collection had just doubled in one day, or more precisely, in one morning.

The people disappeared, the streets turned into one wide street, and the houses were scattered in big groups distant from one another. The car started to climb up a mountain that sat within a cloud. The cloud was so murky that it hid everything. It seemed as if it had drawn into it everything that was in my stomach, and the whirlpool that was created blocked the way. The car advanced slowly, crossing the cloud of my feelings, leaving some of them behind, and advancing toward others.

At one of the bends, I saw glass boxes connected to a rope with people sitting inside of them, and in a combination of panic and excitement I called out to Shaohan, "Look at that!" Shaohan was surprised by my shouting and looked with me at the strange boxes floating in the sky. "That's a cable car," he explained to me in a peaceful voice, but I wasn't able to take my eyes off that amazing thing, until it was hidden by the next bend. "I've never seen anything like that," I said to Shaohan, breathless with excitement. "I also haven't," he answered, "I'd only heard from my uncle who was here once that the cable car takes people to the top of the mountain, to the Buddha. But that ride is too expensive." Shaohan spoke to me while concentrating on the twists and turns in the road. "After we find work," he added, "I promise you that I'll take you for a ride in the cable car."

The way up became even steeper, and the cloud covered the road. It was impossible to see anything, just the gray fog that hid the road. My ears hurt from the steep ascent, and I was cold even though the car windows were closed. I very much wanted to ask Shaohan if he felt like that too, did he also have butterflies, and high waves, and whirlpools that hid the way? These questions stayed stuck in my throat, and I didn't manage to express them in words; I was sorry that I couldn't get an answer for them.

A sign directed us to a parking lot, and we still couldn't see anything. We walked to the sign that led to the Buddha, when suddenly I saw from afar a giant folded leg, and I figured it was part of the statue that we had come to see. I hopped in place, and didn't know if I should run there. Finally, I grabbed Shaohan's hand and pulled him toward the statue. Raindrops started to fall and I was really cold. We ran without stopping and as we got closer, we saw more and more of the enormous statue. We reached the bottom of the staircase that led to the statue. Shaohan noticed that I was very cold, and asked the woman at the entrance to the stairs if it was possible to borrow a coat for the visit to the statue. The woman didn't smile back, but pointed to the counter at the entrance and said, "Ask at the lost and found. It's possible that they have a forgotten coat there." We went quickly to the counter and asked to borrow a coat. The woman behind the counter didn't smile either, apparently the sheer number of visitors and the many questions exhausted them. She took out several sweaters in various colors and said: "There are no coats. Choose from these." Unfortunately for Shaohan, the only sweater that fit him was pink…I chose a dark green one that warmed me immediately.

Two hundred seventy-four steps led up to the statue, and we held hands and started the climb. The butterflies and whirlpools bustling around in my stomach were replaced with heavy breathing, and we had to slow down, but we didn't stop laughing at our new clothes. "The pink sweater looks really good on you," I managed to say to Shaohan between laughing and gasping for air. Though we wanted to get to the top, I was having a hard time climbing all the stairs that from mid-way still seemed to go on forever.

As we got closer, we could see what the murky cloud had been hiding from us. The statue was gigantic, breathtaking, and impressive, and I have never since been able to re-create the intense experience that I felt the first time I stood at its foot and took in its whole size. In our village, the neighbors had a few little Buddha statues at home, no one ever took any religious interest in them; there were no ceremonies, and we didn't learn prayers. Apparently the hard work performed by the people in my village didn't leave them time for prayers. I stood in front of the statue and only wanted to close my eyes and pray that I return quickly to my home in the village.

From the day I was taken from the village I would raise my head each day to the sky and ask to return to my parents— but to who had I directed those requests? I wondered. To who had I prayed when I asked and begged that they come to take me home? And now, when I stood in front of this gigantic creature, sitting with the pleasant face, where it's even possible to see a nice smile, I directed my prayers to it. I got down on my knees and closed my eyes tight; I was alone. I went back to breathing normally, though I still had pain filling my lungs. "Please return me to my parents, please, return me to my parents," I repeated my request over and over. Every once in a while, I opened my eyes and looked at the statue. Drops of rain fell into my eyes and mixed with the tears. Since I had arrived in Hong Kong I hadn't cried, and here all of a sudden I wanted to cry for all the time I had been away from my parents.

The tears and raindrops ran down my face, and I cried soundlessly, directing my silent prayer and cries for help to the statue. Before my eyes, I could see my village, the house, I could smell the foods that my mother cooked, I felt the waiting for my father to come home. I pictured myself and my mother running to him together and jumping up to hug him. Apparently I sat like this for a long time, deep in my daydreams, because when Shaohan asked if I wanted to go down, I saw that he was completely soaked. And suddenly, in the short moment that I looked at him, I was afraid that my prayers would be answered here, on the mountain, that they would go through the statue and reach the place that prayers reach, and I knew that at that point, I would have no choice but to make a difficult decision.

I took deep breaths, I wanted to preserve this moment before the statue. I understood that the choice was mine, and decided to plan everything slowly. The butterflies in my stomach wouldn't help me fly to the village, but I didn't want to release them.

We went down the stairs and every once in a while we looked back and saw the statue move away from us and disappear again into the cloud. When we reached the bottom, I read the signs and asked Shaohan to go to the nearby building to light a stick of incense. I remembered that my mother would sometimes light incense sticks at home and sprinkle the fragrant ash in every corner. After that she would put the lit stick into a container full of ash, where it formed another layer of ash. I'd never understood the ritual, but I remembered that I very much loved the scent of the incense, which was strong and clean.

There were many foreigners walking around the front yard of the temple, among them also monks, whom I recognized by their clothing. Incense sticks cost money, and Shaohan refused to buy them with the little money we had. I walked between the incense clouds that rose from the sticks stuck in the jars in the courtyard, and with tears in my eyes, I breathed in the fragrance of my home in the village.

Immigrants

It was only another week before luck smiled upon us, and it happened when we saw a circle of people carrying protest signs outside the KLM Hotel. I read Shaohan the signs, which said, among other things, "No conditions, no work." Shaohan immediately understood what that meant, jumped at the opportunity, and went into the hotel. I ran in after him, like a shadow. "Good morning," said Shaohan to the reception clerk. "I'm sure you'll be happy to know that we both want to work at your hotel for minimum wage, and we have no demands." The clerk smiled broadly and said, "You're right on time."

The clerk led us down a long hallway and knocked on the last door. I read the sign that said, "Acting Manager."

"Yes, come in," the voice on the other side of the door sounded authoritative. The clerk opened the door and said "Two new workers arrived who say they won't strike."

We went in and sat down in his room. The clerk who accompanied us there went out and closed the door, and left us alone with the manager, who was wearing a fancy gray suit and purple tie.

"Nice to meet you, my name is Tony," began the manager and said, "That's my local name, of course. Who are you?" Shaohan thought for a moment and then said without further hesitation, "We are exactly what you need right now, diligent and efficient workers, and we'll do the work of several people without complaint."

The manager smiled and said: "Immigrants…"

I didn't understand what the word "immigrants" meant, but I understood that he knew that we were from China and not locals.

Shaohan didn't answer, and his smile froze.

"You know what, immigrants?!" The manager continued, "You arrived during the strike, which is ruining the reputation of my hotel and its service. You'll start working, and if you're good, we'll organize you work visas as essential workers within a short time."

Shaohan jumped up from the chair and said excitedly, "Let's go! We'll start now and you'll see that you won't be sorry."

Though confused by the conversation, I too got up and shook hands with the manager, and then he led us to another room. From there they took us to the basement to issue us clean greenish work clothes. The smell of the clothes was especially nice, the feel, a little less. They weren't flexible like other fabrics I knew of. I drew them close to me and looked for the smell of my mother's clothes after they were washed. They didn't have the fragrance I remembered, but the smell of the clean clothes comforted me. The clothes were too big for me, the fabric was stiff, and I knew that other people had worn them before me, but despite all this, I felt clean and even a little dressed up for the first time in years.

Shaohan suddenly appeared wrapped in his work clothes, and looked like a monk who had exchanged his orange clothes for light green. "Are you laughing at my clothes again?" he asked with a smile. Did you see how you look?"

For a few minutes we had a good laugh together; we laughed at each other, and at ourselves. In our laughter was relief from all the tension that had built up over the many days we had spent looking for work.

Shaohan came closer and wiped the tears of laughter from my face. I picked up my hand slowly, but before I could touch his face, he pulled me to him and hugged me tightly. The tears of laughter turned to tears of happiness and excitement, and I had the feeling that they were flowing through my entire body. I hugged Shaohan tight and prayed to myself that this moment would never end.

"Come on, let's go!" called one of the workers in the same work clothes. "I'll show you what you need to do."

We walked after him with hearts pounding, and gradually calmed down. I noticed that John was written on the name tag of a guy who looked Chinese, and I didn't understand why he had a foreign name. In the days that followed, I learned that all the Chinese people in Hong Kong had Western names that they had chosen for themselves, or that their parents had added to their Chinese name. I was a bit surprised by this, because I never thought to change the name that my parents had given me.

We followed John into the elevator, for the first time in my life, but in all the excitement from my hug with Shaohan, and from the new work, I hadn't placed any importance on my first elevator experience, which I would repeat each and every day at work. We went up to the eighth floor. John opened one of the doors on which was written the number 811 and we followed him into the room. "This is a regular room in the hotel," he explained. "Every morning you'll receive a list of rooms that just need to be straightened out, and a list of rooms in which you'll need to clean up and change everything for new guests."

He took a long time explaining what needed to be done: how to make a bed, how to clean the toilets and showers... My heart was pounding. I didn't know what hotel rooms were, but given the Western bathrooms about which I had already found out, and despite the shower with the nice, soft towels, I remembered the books that I had read that described all this. When I had read about them, I had no way of knowing whether or not such things actually existed.

John opened another room, showed me where the cleaning supplies were, and asked me to clean the room while he took Shaohan to the kitchen. I had no problem doing the cleaning, which had been so much a part of my life during the last few years, but the fear of being left alone brought tears to my eyes. Shaohan immediately noticed this, and asked John if I could come with them too. "I'm sorry," John told him, "we must clean the rooms, and I must show you the work in the kitchen. As you both saw, there are almost no workers in the hotel. "I didn't want to hurt Shaohan's opportunity to work, and so I right away stood up straight and announced, "I'm fine, really, you two can go ahead."

As I cleaned, I put any thoughts out of my head, as I had done for all the years at the children's home, if only so I wouldn't think of my fear that I'd again be left alone. I pulled off sheets, collected towels, and emptied the trash into a bag that John had left in the hallway. When I transferred papers from the trash basket to the bag, I noticed that there were little notes written in Chinese. I took out one of the papers and saw that written on it were instructions how to get to a certain restaurant in Hong Kong, apparently by the hotel guest. Since the handwriting was in Chinese, I managed to read it. I stood frozen for a moment and thought that maybe one of the guests that came to the hotel would be from my village or one nearby, and maybe he by chance would know my parents and be able to tell me something about them.

My new mission filled me with hope, and for a long time I worked quickly so that I would manage to clean as many rooms as possible, and find in them as many little notes as possible. Despite the pace of my work, thoughts still got into my head about Shaohan and my feelings for him. What would happen if I found a way to return to my parents? How would I be able to leave him? I decided that I had to tell him the story of my life and that more than anything I wanted to return to my house in the village, but I couldn't find the right words to explain this. The thought of the choice that I would have to make led to a nearly paralyzing stomachache, but I managed to continue working anyway.

When I finished cleaning and straightening all the rooms that had been assigned to me, I sat on the floor in the hallway until John arrived. "Get up, get up!" he scolded. "Never sit on the floor. You should never be caught hanging around doing nothing." The tone of his voice surprised me, but I didn't say anything. I got up and followed him into the room next to where I had been sitting. "Let's see how you cleaned," said John and scanned the room. He checked everything, and finally said, "You work great. If you continue like this, you'll do well here." He gave me a strange-looking key, and said that it opened all the rooms. Then we went down together in the elevator to the basement, where I met Shaohan who was very happy to see me. We sat down and changed our clothes and went out into the street, and only then did I see how late it was. We went to pick up the other guys from their work, and Shaohan talked about our experiences during our first day of work the entire evening.

I just kept quiet the whole time, both because I didn't usually participate in the discussions between the boys and just listened, and also because I was very tired. I was pleased to hear of the plan to rent an apartment for everyone as soon as we received our first salary. Finally, we would be able to sleep comfortably, and not stuffed in the car.

The tiredness did not dispel the fears that overwhelmed me at the thought that I would have to choose between my past and my future. I knew that I was happy then, but that happiness was not complete. Though it was the best thing that had happened to me since I had been in the children's home, I was afraid that because of it, I wouldn't be able to return home. All night I had trouble falling asleep.

The next day I went happily to work at the hotel. I loved working there and I loved putting on my clean work clothes every morning. I was considered a very quick worker, though I lingered in every room to look for notes written in Chinese in the trash and near the bed. I collected everything and read eagerly, hoping to find some sign related to the village or my parents.

The search made the work more challenging, and I didn't rest for a minute. The worker in charge of me was very pleased with my work, and I hoped that he would leave me in that position and not switch me to another so that I would be able to continue collecting information.

Shaohan was working in the kitchen and was in charge of stocking groceries. Every morning he would count all the items in the kitchen and write what needed to be ordered on an inventory sheet. Since he didn't know how to read or write, he had to learn the names of the grocery items according to their Chinese characters, which he copied down.

Shaohan was a responsible worker with lots of energy. He very quickly became friendly with the hotel staff. He always came in with a smile, which stayed on his face all day. He received every request for help with pleasure. He worked very quickly and took no breaks the entire day. He soon got to know all the workers, and asked how they were doing each day. When someone didn't feel well, he volunteered to do their work too. I waited for him to finish both his tasks and those of others before we left the hotel together.

After two weeks, we received our first salary, and after two months, we received a special work visa so we could work at the hotel legally. I had very mixed feelings about this. I understood that my fate was directing me to continue working, to join the boys in their apartment and live in Hong Kong. The thought of this depressed me, and the night that Shaohan wanted to celebrate receiving the visa, heavy feelings weighed me down. Shaohan kept asking me what had happened, and why I wasn't happy, and I avoided giving him a straight answer.

***

Shaohan asked one of the boys to take a day off to find us an apartment. We already knew the city and the subway lines, and Shaohan asked one of the boys to find an apartment in an area far from the center of town, but near a subway station. In a short time, the boy found an apartment with two rooms, a bathroom, shower, and small kitchen. The building was old, but very close to a subway stop. Shaohan sold his car to John from the hotel, and bought mattresses. One double and four single mattresses. Before he gave the car to John, Shaohan used it to bring the mattresses to the new apartment.

"Ming and I will sleep in the smaller room, and you will sleep in the other room," he announced, without bothering to ask me what I thought. Though I was pleased with his decision, I didn't know if it was fair to the other boys. They, however, accepted his decision as if it were obvious, and quickly got settled in their room.

After I cleaned the shower and bathroom, I stood for the first time in my life in a shower with running water. The whole time I lived in the village, my mother would sit me down in a tub and pour water on me with a vessel. Even now when I shower, I rub the back of my ear as my mother did when I was a child. I stood under the stream of water and enjoyed the water sliding down my body. I opened the bottle of shampoo that I had taken from the hotel, and washed my hair. The smell intoxicated me. It was a new smell of freshness, the smell of the future.

Lost and Found

Work became part of the routine of my new life. I loved my freedom, enjoyed the work and was very much appreciated for it. I received both a fair wage and compliments on my hard work and my smile, which I didn't even known I had. I missed almost nothing from my life at the children's home, except for my friend Seyoung, who every time I thought about her I felt great pain, even physical pain, in my stomach, my head, my chest. I thought a lot about Ms. Shuang, about the opportunities she opened up for me when she taught me to read, and I could pass whatever free time there was reading something enjoyable, and dreaming about faraway places.

Many books were left in the hotel rooms, but everything I found I had to put in the lost and found room at the hotel. Most of the books were in English, and I was very sorry that I couldn't read them. Sometimes I found books in Chinese, and I read the back cover or the first page. Every time I held a book in my hand I got very excited. Every book was a world unto itself for me. And I opened each book with uncontrollable curiosity. In the rooms that I only needed to straighten up, I was too shy to open the books and burst into someone else's world – that's why I only ran my hand over the book. My longing for books increased every time I found a book in

Chinese that I could read in a room that guests had left.

I decided to ask John if I could read books during the break or after hours in the lost and found room. John chuckled at this question and said he would be quite happy for me just to take the homeless books to help clear out the room. "And what if someone comes back for a book that he forgot?" John waved his hand dismissively, but I knew that the books were very important to their owners, and therefore, I decided to make a list of all the books in Chinese in the lost and found room, and mark each time which books I took home.

***

The first days that I took books with me, I hurried home and told Shaohan that he could go out and have fun with his friends. I read a book a day, and did not let go of it, not even when I ate. The feeling of freedom brought by reading returned to me with the first book, and I was immediately swept into its imaginary world, or the lives of other people. I floated above the characters, I entered them when I liked them, circulated through their blood system, and I could feel them and identify with them. I visited magical places, cities, villages, towns, and mountains that I knew I would never see, and I learned that the lives of many people could be crueler than mine. I loved books about whole families. I passionately read conversations between mothers and daughters, and I searched in my memory for conversations I had had with my mother.

At first, Shaohan let me read as much as I wanted, but after a week he was pacing around the apartment, and one day, he smiled at me and asked if I would be so kind as to talk to him. He had never read a book in his life, and didn't understand why I couldn't stop. I thought that maybe I made him feel bad that I was more educated than him, but I knew that no matter what, I would never give up reading books. In the end, I asked him to let me read a little every evening, and then I would tell him parts of the book I was reading. Shaohan listened earnestly, sometimes asking questions, and sometimes he asked to make changes. I explained that it was a book and it couldn't be changed.

"Why don't you write yourself?" he asked. His face was serious and he looked me straight in the eye.

"I never thought of that," I said, embarrassed. "I know how to read, but it's hard for me to write." I had never thought to tell my story. Until I heard this question, I had never thought that my story could interest anyone. A few days later, I bought a simple notebook and started to write my story.

***

Most of the books I arranged in the hotel lost and found room had already been to my apartment, and I knew that within a very short time, I would have nothing to read. I asked Shaohan if other hotels would agree to let me read the books that had been forgotten. Shaohan was not keen on the idea and feared that it would draw unnecessary attention, but when he saw my grim face he said, "Ask the concierge who sits in the lobby and helps the tourists, he'll surely help you find books. But be careful not to answer too many questions, because we still don't have citizenship."

At the end of a work day, after I had changed my clothes, I went up to the lobby, to the tourist information desk. Working that shift was a young local boy whom I had seen a few times, but had never spoken to. On his lapel was a tag with his name, Mark Leng, and I understood that he had also received a Western name. His Chinese eyes gave away his origin, but when I spoke to him in Chinese, he smiled in embarrassment and said he didn't speak the language. I stood across from him and tried to remember the few words I had learned in English, but I didn't manage to explain to him what I wanted. Mark went to another one of the reception desk workers, a boy named Steve, and both of them came back to me at the desk. "I'll try to translate your request for him," Steve with the Chinese eyes said. "Thank you," I answered and continued, "please help me find places from which I could borrow books to read. Unfortunately, I can't afford to buy books," I added uneasily.

Steve smiled at me, and instead of telling Mark what I had said, explained to me himself that such a place was called a library, and it was possible to borrow books there, or read them on the spot. Steve spoke English with Mark, and apparently repeated my request, because Mark took out a map of the city in English, and circled three buildings. That evening, I asked Shaohan to come with me to visit the libraries, because I was afraid of the unknown, of the unfamiliar route, of meeting new people and places. I was already used to having someone to protect me and take care of me. I told Shaohan that I wanted him to come with me until I learned how to get there by myself, and to make sure together that the way wasn't dangerous. The next day after work, we rode to the first library.

The Smiling Lady

When we took the subway to the first library on the list, I was glad that Shaohan was with me because I didn't know what to expect. The train stopped at the Tsing Yi station and we were on unfamiliar streets. We got on a bus and traveled to the area called the New Territories. Though the streets in Hong Kong looked like one another, and it was clear that the people walking on the sidewalks were the same people, there was still something strange about this neighborhood. We got off the bus and looked for the building, and after we wandered around the streets for a while, I understood that the main difference was the pungent odors emanating from the food stores, which were different from the smells in the vicinity of our apartment.

We reached the library which was housed in a white building, unlike the brown skyscrapers. The building was shorter but wider than the other buildings, and it looked very inviting; so I had no hesitation entering. A large sign greeted us at the entrance: "Tsing Yi Public Library." I read the sign and didn't understand the meaning of the word "public" because I had nothing to compare it with and didn't know what to expect; I had never been in a library at all, certainly not a public library, and didn't know that the moment I entered this holy sanctuary I would find bliss.

Shaohan opened the door, and there before us was a wide hall with an infinite ceiling. Two women sat behind the counter, and we walked toward them hesitantly. Shaohan was braver and greeted them politely. One of them lifted her head from the book she was reading and smiled at us. We felt awkward and didn't know to what say. The smiling woman picked up her head again. "May I help you?" she asked. I overcame my embarrassment and answered her right away, "Yes, yes." "How can I help?" she asked again. "This is the first time we're here," I answered. "Can you tell us about the library?" The smiling lady stood up, and still smiling, came out from behind the counter and motioned for us to follow her.

A giant glass door separated the lobby from the hall of books, and when we passed through the door behind the smiling lady, a whole new world was revealed. I didn't manage to understand her explanations because I was so excited. I hadn't imagined that there were so many books in the entire world, and certainly not in one place like one public library in Hong Kong. There were rows and rows of shelves with narrow spaces between them, and it reminded me most of the view of the buildings from Victoria Peak, the highest and most famous observation point in the city.

The woman from the counter pointed at the shelves and explained that the books were organized according to topics, and alphabetically within the topics. She mentioned that there were books in Mandarin and Cantonese Chinese and of course many books in English. In the end, she said that it was possible to sit in the library and read any book, but if we wanted to borrow books, we had to sign up for a card and pay for a two-year membership. By this point, I no longer heard or understood anything, because the sights had filled my head, and I could take in no more. I walked up to the shelves to understand the arrangement she had spoken about; there were hundreds of shelves in the library, and dozens of books on each shelf.

"So many books! From where did you receive all these books?" I asked the librarian. "These are books we either purchased or received from generous donors. This isn't the biggest library in Hong Kong, but the books here are certainly on a wide variety of topics," she answered, still smiling.

I looked up at the ceiling, to the space where all the words that people read go up, and the space fills up with infinite life stories. "If you want to read something here, you can sit in the reading corner by one of the tables. When you finish reading, please return the books to the return cart and not to the shelf that you took it from. At the end of the day, we, the librarians, arrange all the books." The librarian's voice was quiet and pleasant. I felt a happiness that I hadn't for a long time, happiness mixed with serenity and clarity. I passed between the shelves, lightly and reverently touching the book covers. Shaohan walked behind me. This was also his first time seeing so many books, but at that moment I didn't understand how uncomfortable the trip to the library had made him feel. It's possible that that visit was what caused him to be angry at my love of books. I took out three books, which I chose because their names had intrigued me, and I asked him to sit with me at the tables so that I could read. Shaohan said that he had nothing to do there, and that he was going to walk around outside.

In the reading corner there were groups of teenage boys and girls sitting by the tables, and grownups sitting alone quietly reading books. Where I was sitting, there were only two people. I still couldn't concentrate on the books because my eyes hadn't had enough of looking around the library. I looked at the shelves again, at the giant hall with the ceiling higher than the ceiling of the hotel lobby. I looked at the people who were reading, and at the young people talking quietly. I remembered that I used to read books to my friends at the children's home in the evening, and even though everyone fell asleep from fatigue after the day's work, I continued to read the book until the end.

That day I didn't manage to read anything in the library, I only sat there and thought of Ms. Shuang, and wondered if she was familiar with libraries like these. She would certainly have enjoyed sitting and reading in such a place. I thought of the books that she gave me at the children's home, first amusing children's books, and later, when my reading had improved, long books for adults. Every once in a while Ms. Shuang would give me a book and announce loudly that it was an important book dealing with the Cultural Revolution, a book that the leader Mao himself recommended that everyone read. I understood that she had no choice but to bring these books to us at the children's home, and therefore I was forced to read them. I would only skim the words with my eyes without internalizing the meaning, and when I finished, I reported loudly, in front of the principal or her assistant, that I had read the amazing book that Mao had recommended we read, and because of that I understood why it was so important that we be there. I said this without meaning it and without really knowing anything, but I understood that that was the price I had to pay to continue reading books. Afterwards, I would continue with the things I was interested in, and didn't speak with Ms. Shuang about those books any further.

**

I have no idea how much time had passed, but suddenly Shaohan returned. He seemed restless. "Are you done?" he asked impatiently. "Can we go home already?" His voice was tough and his face was serious. "Yes," I answered quietly. I'll just return the books I haven't read and we'll go." Despite the disappointment, I tried to placate him.

The entire ride home on the bus Shaohan said nothing, and I, who was floating on a cloud of words, and on the pages of books, noticed this only when we got off at the train station.

"Why are you so quiet?" I asked in an honest attempt to understand.

"It seems to me that you really go too far with this reading stuff," he said angrily. "We need to work and take care of a home, and we have no time for such nonsense." This was once again his unpleasant voice bursting out, which I was already familiar with from the way he acted with his Chinese friends. Though there was a certain logic in his words, his referring to reading books as nonsense offended me.

"Do you think reading is nonsense?" I said in surprise. I wanted to add that he surely thought that because he didn't know how to read, but I managed to stop myself so as not to hurt him.

"Yes, reading books is a waste of time, and I hope that you stop that stupidity and concentrate on me, our home, and work," he muttered angrily, and then he got on the train without allowing me to go in first and sit down. I didn't know what to answer. I didn't want to make him mad, and I was afraid he would leave me. I knew that my life depended on him at that point, and it would be better not to create an argument.

I decided to ignore the insult and just bit my tongue.

When we got home, I saw that the other boys hadn't returned from their day at work. Shaohan sat at the table, and said aggressively, "Have you made anything for supper?"

The question was like a kick in the stomach, and hurt me, and I didn't know how to answer or what to do. I ran to the bathroom and managed to catch my breath. Only there did I understand the significance of the question, and I began to suspect that Shaohan might not be the person I thought he was.

I left the bathroom and announced loudly that I would immediately prepare something for supper. I put a pot of water on the stove, and started cutting up two kinds of mushrooms. When the water started boiling, I put the mushrooms into the pot together with glass noodles that I knew Shaohan liked a lot. I added some spices and waited impatiently for the soup to be ready.

I served Shaohan a full bowl of soup, took only a bit of the liquid for myself. I had no appetite that evening. Shaohan ate in silence with his head down, and didn't look up at me.

"What made you so angry at the library that you are acting this way to me?" I whispered, breaking our silence.

"I am afraid that you will waste time and money on nonsense," he answered aggressively and continued eating. I thought about the notebook I had bought. I hid it in a bag, and wrote in it at night, after Shaohan fell asleep, and his breathing filled the room.

I beg you to let me continue reading," I pleaded. "Reading books saved me in the children's home, and it makes me very happy," I added, with tears in my eyes. "I promise that it won't hurt my work or the jobs I have at home, because I can read a bit before going to sleep."

"I'm not going to give you money for a membership at the library," Shaohan said forcefully. He picked up the bowl to his mouth and gulped the soup.

"I'll pay from my money," I said angrily, trying to hold back the tears. Shaohan didn't answer, he just got up and went to bed.

I didn't fall asleep that night. It was hard for me to see Shaohan as I had discovered him to be that day. The friendly guy that everyone liked, who helps everyone, wasn't there for a minute. I preferred to think that his objection to my reading stemmed from the fact that at that time he still didn't know how to read, but he never admitted that.

***

Many days passed in silent anger. On top of this were a lack of sleep and a feeling of discomfort in the house and at work, and I decided to speak with Shaohan about what had happened, and more importantly, about what would be. I was afraid to hurt him. If it weren't for Ms. Shuang, I also wouldn't know how to read and write, and possibly I also wouldn't know about the world of books. I thought a lot about how to explain myself, and in the end, my feminine intuition led me to decide to hold the conversation after a special supper that I would prepare for Shaohan: his favorite soup, full of vegetables and chunks of fresh chicken.

I returned home before Shaohan, and also before the other guys, who were supposed to return much later, and immediately started preparing the soup. The preparation wasn't long, but each stage was calculated and precise. First I cut the chunk of chicken into thin strips, and this time I made sure to remove all the tendons so that it would be softer. I put the strips in the pot with a bit of warm water so that they would cook before the soup. I cut the mushrooms after wiping them with a towel only, and sliced them very thin. Shaohan had told me once that he loved having the vegetables cut this way, exactly as his mother had done.

I tried to recall my mother preparing food, but I couldn't picture her actually cooking. I remembered the smell in the house whenever I came in to eat, but I couldn't remember the taste of the soup she prepared. I never ate soup the whole time I was in the children's home, and I actually learned to prepare soup only according to Shaohan's descriptions and explanations. I rinsed the bok choy, and put it in water so it would cook with the soup until it boiled. I coarsely chopped the root vegetables and they gave off a strong smell, and when they were all mixed together in the water with the soup, a very pleasant warm fragrance filled the entire apartment.

The smell was unlike the one in my house in the village, because maybe my mother seasoned the soup a bit differently, or maybe time had dulled my sense of smell, but every time that I breathed in the aroma, I tried to identify in it the smell of my mother's cooking. When the soup boiled, I turned off the flame, put the bok choy in a separate dish, and added to the pot the mung bean sprouts and the thick soba noodles that I bought in the medicinal herbs store where I used to buy tea leaves. I covered the pot, and left only a small opening to allow the steam to escape and maintain the fragrance of the soup, which even if it wasn't like the scent of my house in the village, it was definitely the smell of home cooking. For the first time in many days, I felt that I had a home.

Shaohan came home, and unlike the previous days of silence, this time, the aroma of the cooking conquered his pride, and the smile returned to brighten his face. I smiled too, because for the first time, I understood the power of women to control the stomachs of men. He sat down at the table and waited for me to serve him a bowl. Only after he had finished eating two full bowls and all the bok choy that I had put on his plate, and had announced that he couldn't move, only then did I open my mouth and begin to speak.

"I'm sorry that you don't know how to read," I said quickly so as not to regret my words, and immediately explained: "If you knew how to read, you would understand the urge I feel each and every time, you would understand how escaping to the world of books helped get me through difficult days, and how today reading enables me to discover new worlds and be happy."

I paused for a moment, and then continued: "I understand that it is strange for you that I love to read so much, and maybe I also got a little carried away and didn't notice that my reading comes at the expense of our time together, but I want you to understand that reading books is very important to me."

Shaohan understood the tactic. He continued to smile, and the smile turned into roaring laughter. "What happened?" I asked with concern.

Shaohan smiled at me. "What happened?" he asked. "You drug me, make it so that I sit down and can't move, and then you make speeches at me that I cannot take in because the soup went straight to my head..." and he broke out again in rolling laughter that swept me along with it.

We didn't speak again about reading the entire evening. We did not speak about the notebook that I had bought. The notebook was my own private possession, as was my story.

After we finished supper with loud laughter, the tension between us dissipated, and we could continue the evening, and make up in bed. I got into bed first, and removed my clothes under the sheet. Shaohan already knew well every inch of my body, but I still wanted to get undressed and remain covered. The light went out, and I knew that he was on his way to me. I wasn't cold, but my body trembled and contracted anyway. Only when Shaohan's warm skin touched mine did the trembling and contracting stop.

When his lips grabbed my lips and his tongue slipped into my mouth I longed to feel his hands on me. And as if Shaohan had read my mind, his hands climbed up my stomach and moved toward my breasts. When his rough hands pinched my nipples, I felt currents rising and falling in my body, warm pleasant currents that tickled me from inside. I felt that then he must not remove his hands from me. My body started to move to the rhythm of a dance – at first slowly, but very quickly the rhythm grew faster, together with the currents. I moved my hips against him, moved back, and again moved against him and moved back.

The room was dark, but his eyes shone in the darkness. I looked into them deeply, as if to grasp the pleasure in them. Slowly I moved my legs apart, longing to feel him inside of me. The rhythm of our bodies increased, until we worked as one.

In the morning, when we got up together for work, I received an answer from Shaohan that, for the time being, satisfied me: "Once a week, you are free to go to your library, and once a week I get served amazing soup." He smiled at me and laughed.

Local Literature

The smiling librarian who had gotten used to seeing me arrive at the library sat next to me and looked at the pile of books that I put on the reading table. I always put a pile of books next to me, though each time I concentrated on one book from beginning to end. Sometimes I would finish a book after three visits to the library, and sometimes I would finish a short book in one visit.

The librarian returned the books to the pile near me and said, "You always choose to read translated novels. Is that what interests you?" She smiled pleasantly at me.

"I don't know why," I said uncomfortably. "I choose books mainly according to the blurb on the back cover. Sometimes, I skim a few random pages." I hoped that I had answered her question, but she continued to ask why I didn't read local literature. I had never given much thought to my selections. I loved to read the books that took place in countries I had never been to. I loved to read books that took place in countries I wasn't familiar with, I loved to read about things that took place in the past, and about places I would never see. I hadn't thought much before choosing what to read, I thought to myself, but I always found interesting things in every book. I looked at the librarian, and tried again to explain, "I like to know about everything," I said, "and reading foreign books helps me learn about other people and countries that I know nothing about."

The smiling librarian slowly rose, trying to maintain the quiet and not bother the other readers, and disappeared among the shelves. When I arrived at the library the following week, the librarian came right up to me and handed me two books. The books were short, and the language they were written in was indeed different from what I had been reading up until then. I understood them entirely, but the descriptions were strained and limited, as if trying to hide something, and the words that described various events were strangely lacking. I felt that the writer wanted to write but was afraid. However, I felt that I was reading about my neighbors from the village.

I was familiar with the characters, and as such, I was less interested in them. In the characters that appeared in the stories, I found my own way of life, as much as I remembered it, my language and my daily routine, and therefore I didn't understand why it was so important to the librarian that I read them. I returned the books to her after I had finished them, and asked her why she had wanted me to read those books. "I thought you would like to know how writers from your country write, and not only how foreigners write," she answered with a solemn expression. I apparently blushed in embarrassment, because I felt my temperature rise, and beads of sweat break out on my forehead. I didn't dare tell her about my past, and fell silent. I still feared that they would throw me out and return me to China if I were found out about by the authorities. In her wise eyes, I saw that without words she understood where I had come from and why I was afraid.

***

The next time I came to the library, I took an atlas and tried to find certain places I had recently read about. The librarian waved hi to me, and after about an hour, she approached me with a book with a colorful cover. "I looked for it especially for you," she said and sat down with me, smiling as usual.

"What is the book about?" I asked and looked for the blurb on the back cover.

"It's an autobiography by a Chinese man who fled to the U.S.," she said. When she saw my questioning look, she explained, "An autobiography is the life story of an author written by himself, and this book contains the tragic life story of a simple fellow whose only sin was that he practiced the Falun Gong. Do you know what that is?" she asked expectantly.

"No," I answered, and waited, curious for an explanation.

"It is a spiritual practice that is considered very healthy. It's similar to Tai Chi, which you've probably heard about here." The librarian paused for a moment, and then continued with an explanation: "The authorities in China prohibited its citizens from practicing it after it generated huge gatherings of practitioners. Anyone who continued to practice it was imprisoned, and any written or recorded material on it was confiscated by the regime. Chai Li, the author, was among those imprisoned, and when he managed to flee to the U.S., he published his story."

I read the story[2] from beginning to end without moving.

---

2   The writer is not describing the plot of the book, but the plot of the movie **Free China: The Courage to Believe**, Michael Perlman's 2013 documentary film.

Only my hand moved to wipe the tears spilling down my cheeks. The book revealed to me for the first time the aggressiveness of the Chinese regime. I saw that it wasn't just me who had been sent for re-education, rather, everyone had undergone educational and physical terror during that period. The book reviewed what had happened after the period of Mao's rule, the failure of the Cultural Revolution, and the cruel appropriation of liberties from the citizens. Whatever was even vaguely suspected of being an anti-regime organization was eradicated. This was true for the mass spiritual practice that gained popularity throughout China. I understood why the librarian had given me that book to read, and I was embarrassed by the fact that she knew so much about me without my having told her a thing.

***

Chai Li's book left its mark on every part of my body: on my hands, my eyes, my head, my stomach, and on every internal organ. For many days, I could not stop thinking about the horrific descriptions of what had happened to the Chinese people and to Chai Li himself. I knew that this terrifying story was true, mainly because it reminded me so much of life at the children's home, and I knew well that such cruelty was impossible to invent.

In the book, Chai Li wrote that Mao was on the level of a god for the Chinese people, and I thought of his pictures hanging on the walls of the large hall in the children's home. Though I had known about Chairman Mao since my childhood in the village, I had never heard good or bad about him. My parents and the other people in the village were simple people, workers of the land, who lived their daily lives without troubling their minds about the regime. Only afterward did I understand that Mao had wanted to destroy Chinese tradition, give up the old values, and create a new China. The great adoration of him stemmed, apparently, from the hope that something good would happen. But while the good was slow to come, his revolution took hold. The prohibitions increased, freedom was taken from the citizens, everyone worked for the regime, and there was no place for opponents. The Communist movement ruled by force, and Mao's successor, Deng Xiaoping, though he declared that he wanted the best for the citizens and began to establish contacts with the West, he was actually cruel to anyone who tried to express an opinion against him or his party. He acted violently and used soldiers and the military to suppress demonstrations or disperse gatherings. Every association was declared forbidden, and the citizens did not really have complete freedom. The greatest pain inflicted on the Chinese people was in their being cut off from their traditions. Deng Xiaoping announced that "to get rich is glorious" and forgot the value of human life on the way to achieving that goal.

To become rich at the expense of human life is cruelty, I thought to myself. My life in our village was happy, this I remembered throughout the years. We did not have abundance, but there was much warmth and love – the love of my mother and father and friends all around.

From Chai Li's story, I also learned about what happened in Tiananmen Square. The spontaneous demonstration which was joined by more than a million Chinese in protest of corruption in the regime, ended in a tremendous disaster in the killing of thousands of citizens demonstrating in and around the square. I felt that if I had been there, I surely would have joined the demonstration in the square against the regime. I saw myself holding a sign near my friends, with the police approaching us. Yet I stood in my place, and did not run away. They had taken me once—and that time I had fled.

Chai Li's only crime, like millions of Chinese people who were detained and sent to work camps for years, was that he practiced Falun Gong. From reading his book, I learned that Falun Gong was a spiritual practice combining meditation and physical movements. It was based on the values of Buddhism and upheld the three principles of meditation: truth, compassion, and tolerance. Not one of these values was enshrined by the Chinese regime, which did not foresee the development of Falun Gong throughout China.

Falun Gong turned into a popular movement based on a positive spiritual approach to life—the desire to live a peaceful and healthy life. In the movements performed by practitioners of Falun Gong was a combination of body and soul, mutual and fruitful influence. The practitioners felt peace and spiritual strength. The Falun Gong movement soon spread across China, and the sight of tens of thousands of practitioners gathered in public places worried the Communist party. The power of the large crowds that joined together brought the government to fear rebellion, and it therefore made a sweeping and unequivocal resolution prohibiting practice of the system or owning anything related to it. Whoever did not obey and continued to practice was considered a member of a bad and harmful cult, and was sent for "re-education."

Chai Li was among those detained after refusing to stop practicing. First he was taken into custody. In his book, he described how he and all the detainees were forced to sit hunched over every day for 15 hours, and he wrote about the electric shocks he received to cause him to admit that the practice of Falun Gong was not a good thing. After his detention, Chai Li was sent to work at a factory and sewed dolls and slippers for American companies. For the entire period of his imprisonment, he was forced to contend with the harsh and incessant brainwashing of the prison guards. Unlike many others who did not withstand the pressure and broke down, mainly family members who preferred to declare that the practice of Falun Gong was bad and promise to abandon it, Chai Li did not break down and worked at the factory for a long time.

***

The descriptions in Chai Li's book brought me back to the village of my birth. What had happened to my parents? I wondered. Had they stayed in their little house and continued with their lives, or had they too been taken to work camps or for re-education? I wanted to believe that that had not happened, but inside of me was the feeling that I couldn't argue with, a sharp and clear feeling that I had remained alone, and they hadn't come to take me because they had also been taken by representatives of the regime. This understanding made it a bit easier for me to accept that my parents had abandoned me.

At some point, Chai Li decided to begin a hunger strike. "I am left with no choice but to take a hunger strike upon myself, any other way plays right into the hands of the cruel government officials," he announced. The prison guards tied him to the bed and force-fed him via tubes stuck into his nose. After a time, Chai Li felt that his health was weakening, and he stopped the strike, "I broke down, spiritually and physically. I was unable to stand the physical pressure of the attempts to feed me through tubes inserted into my body," he told in his book, whose pages I quickly drank up, my heart pounding.

Though Chai Li's health had degenerated, he was still performing forced labor sixteen hours a day, every day. Chai Li asked to send letters to his family, but the prison authorities did not allow him to do this. When I read this I remembered the letters that I had given to Ms. Shuang and believed that she had sent them, but given what I read in the book, I was afraid that my parents were already not in the village to receive them.

The work camps in China, officially known as "laogai", were designed for the re-education of the millions of Chinese people who arrived there. We were taken to a children's home, but the children's home also quickly became a work camp.

One of the methods by which to obtain the obedience of the prisoners in the camps was the threat that they would hurt the family members of the prisoners – parents and children alike. Many did not stand up to these threats and surrendered. I could also understand anyone who surrendered, anyone who asked them not to hurt their children or family. Those that broke down were sent to serve as preachers against the Falun Gong, and supervise the investigations and torturing of those who had not yet surrendered. Every word that I read filled me with tremendous anger. I was ashamed that I was a part of this and that I had been born in a place where people were doing such things.

After three years, Chai Li was released following the intervention of Western countries, mainly the U.S., which led the struggle for the release of these prisoners after they received information on what was happening in the camps from

citizens who had managed to escape. "My personal story and
the terrible stories of many others, I committed to disseminate
in the world to bring all this to an end," Chai Li promised, and
his story was indeed publicized in many countries. In the end,
he brought pressure to bear on the Chinese government to
release the many prisoners that remained in the work camps.

I read this and was filled with rage, which was soon
replaced with gratitude. I had also been exposed to Chai Li's
story and that of the Falun Gong with the assistance of the
librarian. I finished reading the book, and I remained filled
with rage, wonder, hope, and above all, strong longing. My
desire to return to the village of my birth and see what had
happened to my parents, became all at once something that
I could no longer ignore. I knew that Shaohan was opposed
to my returning there, but it was clear to me that I could not
continue my life without knowing what had become of my
parents, and without their knowing that I was a free person.

I got up and approached the librarian, who as usual was
smiling, even though she saw my teary eyes. I approached her
in fear, but then a loud cry burst from my throat. I hugged
her with all my might, seeking support. The librarian hugged
me tight. "Let's sit down, calm down," she said to me gently,
consolingly, and sat me on a chair. "I had no idea that you
would react like this, maybe I should have warned you…" I sat
until I stopped crying, and then I hurried home to Shaohan.

***

I have read many books in my life, but that book will always be
the book that influenced me more than any other, that molded
my life. From the moment that I read it, a day did not go by

that I did not think of my family or of my friends and what had happened to us.

The weeks that followed in the library were the hardest for me. From reading enjoyable novels, I had moved to the obsessive search for Chinese works by authors who escaped to freedom. Since there were not many of these, I could quickly return to what I had been reading before, but the stamp of the painful stories I read remains on me until today, and it is unlike the pain of my memory. It is a collective and cruel pain. Beyond my own private pain, it holds inside it the pain for a glorious culture stolen by a regime that sought power for itself instead of giving it to the good people that it was stealing it from.

Every time I went there, the smiling librarian brought me a stack of books. It seemed that she too wanted to re-educate me, but it appeared that her intentions were good. To retain my love of books, I would read one book that I chose and one book that she chose, reading both Western novels and history books, thought, and political science. I learned all the methods of the regime, and I understood the rights and obligations of the citizens.

I still didn't know what I would do with all this knowledge, but in the meantime, I continued with my routine—the work at the hotel, my once a week visit to the library, being at home with Shaohan, cooking our suppers, and the expectation that he would come to bed and that again a stormy passionate dance would unfold. It was a routine that I created for myself, I had the right to decide, and each day I was excited by the pleasure in my freedom. I wasn't yet 20, but I felt grown up. I was no longer a teenager, but a woman.

Spasms

Though I longed to return home to my parents in China, I wanted with all my heart to stay with Shaohan. I felt good with him. I was supposed to be smiling, going to work, and for the first time feel that I was in charge of my fate. I already should have known that I could support myself and buy myself everything that I needed to live respectably. I could have lived this way with Shaohan and we could have worked together to build our life in the new place, but in my thoughts, I was somewhere else. I was caught in a struggle between my desire to return home, and my desire to remain free with Shaohan.

Each morning I woke up in bed in the small apartment, next to Shaohan, thanks to whom I was free. Each morning I had spasms in my stomach, when I looked at him, and each time I was excited all over again when he looked in my eyes as soon as he opened his. But these spasms were a sign of apprehension, not just excitement. The daily spasms were my reminder of the passion that could not yet be doused, the passion to return home, to the smell of my mother. My stomach cried out what my head sought not to think about.

The sadness penetrated my body and soul, hit all the places that had recovered from the injuries of the children's home, and wrapped around my freedom to work for a decent salary.

It whirled my feelings for the man that had found me, picked me up, and loved me. I was Shaohan's first partner, and I felt his fear clearly every time he wanted to get close to me, to touch and caress me. I finally felt that someone cared about me, that I was important to him. This was the feeling I had longed to feel all those cursed years of my imprisonment in the children's home. I remembered a trace of that feeling from my mother, and during that entire period in the children's home, I got to feel just a pinch of it from Ms. Shuang – and only in a few unforgettable cases. The passion to return to my mother and start all over in my birthplace was mixed with my desire to stay with Shaohan, and every morning, my stomach contracted in a spasm of pain.

***

One evening, after we finished the supper that I had prepared for everyone, I went to take a shower. I knew that I needed to speak with Shaohan about my dilemma, but I feared his reaction. Truthfully, I knew how he would react, though I couldn't imagine its intensity, or its effect on me. The time that we were passing together didn't make anything easier for me, and as the water flowed over my body, I felt that my life was flowing furiously, and enveloping me in warmth.

The drops brought back memories of the cold cups of water that Seyoung and I had splashed on each other to clean the sweat and dirt after a days' work in the rice fields. The cold water didn't always do the job, and I remembered breathing Seyoung's body odor every night.

I wanted to smell her body again, I wanted to tell her what had happened to me, to share with her my deepest feelings.

Since I left the children's home, I hadn't had a friend like her, a friend that was a part of me, and I knew that I wanted to return also for her. My new life had not caused me to forget her, in fact, sometimes I longed for her more than for my parents.

The water continued to flow over my body, and at the same time, thoughts passed through my head about Seyoung: the fact that I had replaced her with Shaohan so naturally; cuddling up with her any time we were cold had turned into a lover's embrace with him; I remembered our nightly talks after an exhausting day, talks that inspired and revived me, and I thought with pain how now I was avoiding discussions with Shaohan, and not allowing him access to my thoughts.

Seyoung knew everything, she understood me before I spoke. I had never dedicated myself to anyone as I had to Seyoung. Many times I had been able to hold on just because of her, many times when I broke down I didn't want to disappoint her, and I pretended that I was strong. I didn't notice how long I had been in the shower until there was a knock on the door that awakened me from my thoughts. "Is everything okay?" asked Shaohan.

"Yes of course, I'll be right out," I answered.

My skin had shriveled because of the time I had spent under the hot water. I smiled at my fingers that had wrinkled up from the water, just as there were wrinkles every day from picking rice in the water. Shaohan was waiting for me outside the bathroom, and followed me to our room.

"You were in the shower for over an hour. What happened?" he asked and gave me a penetrating look.

"I was thinking of my friend from the children's home, whom I miss very much, and I didn't notice the time."

I didn't tell him everything, but in contrast to his usual way, this time Shaohan did not give up.

"You never told me what you went through," he said, and I heard the anger in his voice. "Maybe you could start sharing it with me, after all, I am your boyfriend!" I felt sadness spread throughout me. Suddenly I understood that the place where I had been imprisoned all those years had taken my true identity from me, had accustomed me to keep quiet. This was the first time that Shaohan had described our relationship in words, and this simultaneously moved and hurt me. I understood that I could no longer hide my past from him.

That night, we didn't sleep at all, despite the fact that we knew we needed to be alert for work in the morning. I told him everything, only after asking him first to listen, and only then react. I told him about my birth village and my parents, and he listened quietly, smiling at the story of the wagon that was built for us, and enjoying the way that I described my colorful house. When I told him of the night when I was taken to the children's home together with the children of the night, Shaohan became serious and looked surprised. When I described the beatings and the torture I had undergone after my failed escape attempt, I saw tears in his eyes. He tried to get close to me and put out his arm, but I refused this gesture and asked that he first let me finish my story.

I continued to tell him about my friends at the children's home, about Deshi whom I had promised to protect but had let him down. I told him about the three Changs in the village, about Hu-Vi, Jiali, and Liang who would play the serial story game with me on the few evenings that they still had energy after the day of work in the fields, and mainly I told him about Seyoung who had been my friend and sister. Sometimes she treated me like a protective mother, and sometimes like a spoiled child, but most of the time, she was my soulmate. After that, I told him how my life had changed when Ms. Shuang came, as she had taught me to read and had given me books.

I wanted to tell him everything I had been through, but I didn't want to get to the reason for which I had to tell him everything. I had the feeling that I was adding details and making the descriptions longer, but the knowledge that when I finished speaking I would have to tell him that I wanted to return to my village caused me to speak without stopping.

I looked at the clock whose hands had advanced faster than the pace of my story, and I knew that I was near the end. My throat was hoarse, but I didn't want to get up for water; I was afraid that if I got up, I would decide not to say everything that was on my mind, and so I continued talking. I had never spoken so much, and until then I had never felt that I didn't want to stop talking.

Shaohan was very attentive. I was happy that my life and my past interested him so much that most of the time he chose to keep quiet and not bother me with questions. I became filled with fear as I continued talking: would he be so attentive when he heard that I wanted to leave Hong Kong? The thoughts mixed with the words that I said, and while I was talking I tried to decide how to end and how to say the last sentence, hoping that it wouldn't be the last.

We were lying down facing each other, sometimes changing position so as not to fall asleep, but we did not touch at all, as if the stories of my past were being screened before his eyes, but he couldn't be part of them. Suddenly I wanted to get close to him and touch him. I wanted to be closer to him than ever. What could I say so that he would understand? How would I say it to the man who had picked me up exactly at the moment that I had again been taken from a familiar place to a foreign place, at the moment that I had again been deserted, at the moment when I believed that no one wanted me or cared about me? How would I tell him the truth so that there would not be a raging river between us? I knew I had to cross this river, but would Shaohan put out his arm and help me cross, or would he leave me on the opposite bank?

The night continued, and my stories were almost finished, and I knew that at the end I had to tell him I wanted to return home. Shaohan asked me every once in a while if I wanted to continue the next day, because if we stayed awake any longer, we wouldn't be able to function at work. But I couldn't stop and continued and told him about the trip to Hong Kong with the driver who had deserted me in the waiting room, and about the escape, and about meeting him and his friends.

In the end, after having spoken for many hours, I said softly "I want to return to the village." Shaohan looked at me icily. After that, his face turned red, and the color became darker when he clenched his fists and tensed up his entire body. I was frightened by this, but I didn't move. I continued to look at him, waiting for him to talk. I didn't dare say anything, certainly not to explain, because it was already clear that he had understood and, as I wondered what to do, he turned his back toward me. I don't know if he fell asleep, because I only cried, warm tears flowed from my eyes.

I didn't dare touch him or ask him to turn around. I didn't understand how he could fall asleep and leave me crying next to him, when I needed stroking and understanding. Though I had imagined that Shaohan would be angry to hear what I wanted, his reaction was beyond anger. He disappeared. A dark thought suddenly froze my heart: after I had lost my parents and my friends from the children's home, now I had also lost Shaohan.

I cried over my fate, over the way it always took me one step forward and the next minute threw me back. I knew I wouldn't manage to fall asleep; I wanted the sound of my weeping to break Shaohan's heart and cause him to talk to me. I preferred that he be angry at me, that he scream, that he say something. I was sure that his friends in the other room could hear my crying, but I knew that none of them would dare come to our room to ask what had happened. I lay in bed worn out from crying, but I didn't manage to stop crying and fall asleep. I looked at Shaohan sleeping next to me – his body didn't move, only his chest rose and fell to the rhythm of his measured breathing.

In comparison, my breathing was very quick, and the pace of my thoughts even quicker. I had the feeling that I was lying in bed with a strange man. How could I think that I would want to spend the rest of my life with him? I had known so many disappointments in my short life, and this was the hardest of all. The crying caused me to gasp and cough, but nothing disturbed Shaohan's calm breathing.

I looked at the clock in the hope that time would move fast, and it would already be morning. I continued to sob until it was time to get up for work.

***

When the alarm clock rang, Shaohan got up slowly from the bed and walked heavily to the bathroom. He didn't even glance at me. I waited for him to return, and I too went to wash my face. When I returned to the room, I stood at the doorway and watched Shaohan get dressed. He was concentrating completely on putting on his shoes, and didn't acknowledge my presence in any way, as if I were transparent. I too got dressed, skipped breakfast, and we all went out to the subway. No one talked, it was as if they knew from Shaohan's body language that he was angry and thus they had decided not to get involved. The entire subway ride I tried to catch Shaohan's glance, but he had chosen to cover his eyes with sunglasses and block his view of me. A few minutes later, Shaohan and I got off at the hotel station, and walked side by side like two strangers with only the path in common. We did not exchange a word, not even a goodbye when we each turned in the direction of our respective work at the hotel.

I changed into my work clothes and started to clean and arrange the rooms. My movements were slowed by fatigue and disappointment. There were tears in my eyes the entire day, and I just wanted to see Shaohan and explain to him that my desire to return to the village was what had kept me going all those years at the children's home. I wanted him to understand that I really wanted to stay with him, that I hadn't wanted to choose between him and my parents, but that I had no choice, and had to return to the village and see them.

That day, I threw out all the papers I found in the rooms without sorting through them, without looking for notes that would remind me of home. I was paralyzed by sadness, and didn't know how I would be able to start talking to Shaohan. During work, despite my complete exhaustion, I planned my actions: I would work a few more weeks and save enough money so I could travel back. I didn't know what they would do to me when I tried to cross the border into China, but I decided to ask the hotel manager to give me a letter stating that I had been working for him on a permanent basis, just in case I got into trouble. I thought to go after work to the bus terminal to find out about the trip to the village. I remembered that there was no bus that rode directly to the village, but if I got as close as possible to it, I could continue on foot. Time moved slowly, my eyes brimmed with tears, and I didn't know whether Shaohan would wait for me at the end of the day.

***

Fortunately, there was no room inspection that day. I didn't remember how well I had cleaned—I worked like a robot and thought only of Shaohan, my parents, and the conversation the night before. The best things in my life were making my chest hurt. I thought to myself that the pain that accompanied me throughout that day would surely never disappear, and I would have to get used to living with it; this pain was a gift from my fate, the fate that gave me the freedom to choose. Until that day, I had had a life without choices, I hadn't chosen what happened to me, and so I hadn't felt the pain caused by the mistaken choices, but I still didn't want to return to a life without freedom of choice.

I just had one more room and I knew that Shaohan had already finished his work. To the pain in my chest were added my heartbeats, which were so strong that I was afraid my heart would jump out of my chest and fall on the carpet that covered the floor and walls of the hotel. I even smiled at the thought that it wouldn't be me who would have to clean the blood stains dirtying the rugs. While this thought was going through my mind, I also imagined my heart jumping from my body, falling onto the carpet and rolling in the hallway, and I was still standing and watching it, and in the room that I was cleaning, the television was on and there they were reporting about a young girl working in a hotel whose heart had fallen out of her body while she worked. The reason for this case was being investigated, said the television reporter, and I yelled noiselessly: "I had to make a choice!"

I finished cleaning the last room and hurried to the basement to change my work clothes and leave. Sweat soaked my body, and my heart was still pounding. During all the years that I wanted to return to the village, even when I had tried to escape, I didn't really understand what freedom was, and I didn't know how to seek it. Only there, in Hong Kong, when I understood that my freedom was real and absolute, did I discover that it also comes at a price.

I went out the back door designated for hotel employees. Shaohan stood in front of me, exactly in the place where he always waited for me every day. I couldn't look at him, so I looked down at my shoes and walked toward him. Since I couldn't see anything, my head hit him when I reached him. I stopped in front of him and couldn't control the tears streaming down my face. Shaohan took hold of my shoulders and waited for me to lift my head. We stood there quietly for a while. I lifted my head slowly until my eyes met his, and through the tears, I could see that he was smiling. I was relieved, and the flow of tears grew stronger.

"I thought about what you told me," said Shaohan in a quiet voice.

I straightened up in the hope that he would say that he had thought it over and had understood me. "I want you to stay here and marry me." He added, "I want you to be my wife, and for us to be together forever. I don't want you to return to China."

I looked at him in surprise, and he hugged me warmly and placed a soft kiss on my lips. My heart pounded with excitement, and in the days that followed, I didn't talk with Shaohan about my wish to return home. Before that there were the preparations for the wedding that clouded my senses and filled my time, pushing the plans to return to the village of my birth out of my head.

We both knew exactly where we wanted to hold the ceremony: at the temple next to the Big Buddha. In addition to our close friends, we decided to invite a few friends from the hotel. I invited the rest of the housekeeping staff, and of course our manager, and Shaohan invited his friends from the kitchen. However, despite our attempts to be somewhat discrete about it, the rumor spread, and we decided that anyone who wanted to come, and wasn't supposed to work at the same time, was invited to the ceremony at the temple. Though the memory of that terrible morning when he wouldn't look at me didn't leave me, Shaohan and I were very happy. Every morning I stopped the process of waking up for a second, and didn't open my eyes right away, as I used to do at the children's home. I gave myself a few seconds alone in the dark, seconds where I saw nothing except my words, the words that come out into the room and ask that he understand me, that he understand what I went through and, more than that, that he know who I wanted to be. And every morning I saw Shaohan's captivating smile, and I smiled too.

In the days leading up to the ceremony, I felt as if I were floating above the earth. My movements were soft and flexible, and I stood up straight everywhere I went. I held my head high in pride. My soul had finally relaxed, and was resting on soft carpets of happiness and pleasantness. I felt that I was at home in a place that I had made with my own hands, out of free choice, and the memory of my mother in the little village of my childhood was fading, like the memory of my good friend Seyoung.

***

One morning, John the manager called me and asked me to come with him to the lost and found room. "There are some clothes here that were left by hotel guests that were never claimed," he said. "Look around, maybe you'll find a wedding dress or a suit for your future husband." Tears of gratitude welled in my eyes, and I couldn't stop thanking him. The fact that he thought that I would need clothes that I couldn't afford, and came up with a solution, moved me greatly. Generosity cannot be taken for granted. John, who was embarrassed at this outpouring, excused himself and left me there alone.

The clothes were thrown in piles, folded carelessly. I saw that it would take time until I found something suitable, so I returned there after work, with Shaohan. Each of us stood next to a pile and started to look, but in a few minutes, Shaohan started to throw clothes at me. At first I thought that he wanted to show me what he had found, but soon a clothing war broke out between us: shirts, pants, dresses, and lots of underwear flew in the air and landed on the floor of the storeroom in one large pile. Shaohan knocked me over onto the pile of clothes and for a long time we lay in each other's arms, breathing heavily.

"The clothes here are very tempting," Shaohan finally said, "but I prefer that we buy new clothes for the wedding. I wouldn't want to wear someone else's history." I tried to convince him that that would be expensive, and there were many nice things in the room, but in my heart I was happy with his decision, because I knew that it was a special day for us, and I had never bought a new dress for myself.

For a week, we went every day to look for our wedding clothes. We very much enjoyed wandering around in the stores. There were days when we tried on dozens of outfits, and didn't like anything, but even if we liked something, the high price prevented us from buying it. After about a week of searching at the stores and tailors all over Hong Kong, who sew for everyone both everyday clothes and more special clothes, we found a little store on a narrow street far from the crowds walking around town, where a pair of tailors agreed to sew us clothes made to order at a price we could afford.

Shaohan chose to wear pants and a jacket of dark blue fabric that was a bit shiny, and in that suit he suddenly looked mature and serious to me. Together we chose him a light blue shirt with white buttons. I wanted him to add a tie, but in the end we decided against it. I chose light yellow fabric from which they sewed me a dress that clung tightly down to my waist, and from there it widened like a half-opened umbrella and fell to the floor. I still have that dress in a sealed plastic bag, and every time I come across it I remember how young we were.

Tina, the housekeeper who was my partner in cleaning the rooms almost every day, offered that on the day of the wedding, I would go to her sister's hairdressing salon to do my hair like a bride, and that would be her present. I was so moved at hearing this offer that I hugged her for a long time, something that surprised both of us. Tina always asked how I was, and I always listened to her funny stories, but we had never had any physical contact like a hug. The embrace and excitement shook me so much that I couldn't stop crying for the rest of the day.

The entire hotel staff was involved in our wedding, also because the event became a field trip to the temple for the workers. It was decided unanimously that the younger workers would be the ones who would have to stay and work. A spirit of holiness prevailed in the hotel, and it seemed that the guests were also happier.

***

One morning, a few days before the official wedding day, the hotel manager called Shaohan into his office. Shaohan was afraid that all the commotion over the wedding was distracting the workers from their jobs, and that the manager had called him in to scold him. On rare occasions, Shaohan went to the manager's office, only when the manager wanted to ask him to provide special treatment for a particular guest. Shaohan was always pleased to receive such tasks because it allowed him to spend several days away from the work routine in the kitchen.

This time he was worried when he went into the manager's office. "Sit," the manager said to Shaohan, and his tone of voice gave no clue as to whether he was angry or not.

"Unfortunately, I won't be able to come to your wedding ceremony," the manager said, "because I have a lot of work."

Shaohan interrupted him and mumbled, "No problem, sir, that's okay…"

The manager looked at him with great patience and smiled. "Still, in appreciation for both of your dedicated work at the hotel, I would like to give you a present on the occasion of your wedding." The manager paused for a moment, and then continued, "I have decided to book the grand suite for you for your wedding night, and with all my heart, I wish you only happiness in your life together." Shaohan froze when he heard this. That evening, when he told me about the manager's present, I again couldn't stop the tears.

Time moved on, the days passed, the hours flew by, and our wedding day arrived. Our friends and roommates had already bid us farewell, but not before expressing their warm wishes for us, each in his own way. They rented a small apartment near us, and the entire apartment was at our disposal—the small living room, that until that day had been our friends' bedroom, the kitchen and the shower—we would return to all of these married. That day we did not go to work. We stayed in bed, and didn't know what to do first. We tried to imagine the ceremony, and Shaohan said that his friends surely would do anything to make him laugh at the ceremony. "Look into my eyes the entire ceremony," I said, "that way you won't laugh." Shaohan laughed out loud and said, "I'll try."

For hours, we described to each other how the ceremony would be. I described to Shaohan how he would walk in, kneel before the Buddha, drink and eat with the guests, and Shaohan joined the game and described me arriving at the temple, receiving the guests, pouring the wine. That was our way to get over the excitement, and let time pass until we got up to get organized for the big day.

I arranged to meet with my friend from work at her sister's salon at two, and then I would return home to get dressed. It was decided that Shaohan, who only needed to get dressed, would stay at home and continue to describe to himself how his ceremony would be that would take place in a few more hours, to pass the time and relieve the tension. Besides this, he was to book a taxi to take us to the cable car, because in honor of the wedding, we would be going up to the temple and statue by cable car. The excitement for the ride in the cable car was mixed with the emotions from the ceremony, and our eyes sparkled with happiness and anticipation.

When I got to the salon, all the workers greeted me with big smiles. Tina's sister pulled my hair back in hundreds of hidden pins, and when I looked in the mirror, I didn't recognize myself—I saw a seemingly young, awkward girl, with hair done in a perfect circle around her head, and her face gently made-up. When I got home, I was greeted by Shaohan's surprised look. After I put on the dress and stood before my groom, I tried very hard not to have the tears in my eyes run down my cheeks and ruin the makeup.

The whole way in the taxi, I hoped that the thought of my parents wouldn't cross my mind. I wanted to be happy on this day, and not feel the pain pinching my stomach. I made great efforts not to think about them, but only of other things— the suite awaiting me and my new husband, the children we would bring into the world. I looked at the crowded city, which disappeared on the way to the cable car, and I smiled the whole way to hide the pain I felt with my loved ones in China. How could I get married without my parents? How could I celebrate without my friend Seyoung, and without the children of the night, who were like brothers and sisters to me? But even these thoughts that wandered to the village and back to me and stayed with me on that day did not ruin the happiness and excitement of the day.

The taxi stopped next to the cable car, and when we got out of it, the excitement was replaced with fear of the box hanging in the air. "I had to get married so I could take you for a ride in the cable car," Shaohan said with a laugh, while I howled with fear.

We sat side by side in the cable car. Across from us was a pair of tourists that smiled at us and probably congratulated us, but we didn't understand their language. I held Shaohan's hand as if it were a life rope, in case the cable car fell. I felt the car move off the ground, and swing from the cable above us. Shaohan laughed happily, while I wore a forced smile. The ride in the cable car took about twenty minutes, but to me it seemed like an eternity. I looked down and saw all the islands around, the hiking trails climbing to the mountain, I even saw little people walking on the paths and going up the hundreds of steps on the way. There were times when my stomach turned over, and I was sorry that we hadn't climbed to the top, and there were moments when I enjoyed the landscape exposed as the cable car rose higher. First the urban view and skyscrapers fell farther and farther away, and their place was taken by uninhabited green mountains scattered in the murky sea. As we went higher, we could see a more and more varied landscape. Many islands of many different sizes were scattered underneath us. The sight was like a large puzzle with many pieces that needed to be put together to create a continuum of land. The sea surrounding the islands seemed from above like an opaque metallic surface; it had no depth or transparency. Many tourists in the hotel had told me that they had seen pink dolphins in the water, but my efforts to see anything in the water below were to no avail.

The cable car stopped at the top of the mountain, and in contrast with our previous visit, this time there was no fog covering the mountain, and the Buddha statue was visible from afar.

Ancestor Worship

We walked to the temple on the path leading up to the entrance. On both sides of the path were giant tin containers into which visitors would put lit incense sticks. Thick smoke spread all over, and the strong smell of the incense penetrated my nostrils. When I tried to remember the smells of the incense from my house in the village, a heavy cloud fell upon me.

Shaohan apparently noticed that my steps became unsteady, and he hurried to hold my arm tightly so I wouldn't fall. I closed my eyes and imagined my father holding me and walking with me to the temple. My mother waited for me inside with my girlfriends from the village, and with the neighbors who had arrived. The neighbors' faces were blurry; apparently I already couldn't remember all their features, or perhaps the tears in my closed eyes blurred the faces of the people. My father held me tightly, and I didn't want to open my eyes and find out that I was going inside without him.

"Be careful, there's a step here," Shaohan whispered in my ear exactly when I opened my eyes. I smiled at him from behind the tears, and kept myself from bursting out crying.

The smell of the incense accompanied us inside the temple. We took our shoes off in the entrance and entered with a bow. The pungent smell of the incense outside was replaced by the scent of delicate fruity incense. Shaohan's friends stood in a row and greeted us, and fulfilled the parents' role of collecting the red envelopes that are customarily given to the new couple. I remembered the weddings I had attended in the village as a little girl. The parents of the bride and groom were always there to greet the guests and the couple as they entered. In the village, it was customary to hold a procession consisting of all the people of the village that went from the house of the bride to the house of the groom. Then the families would unite, and the whole ceremony would take place around the parents. At our wedding, we were both alone.

In the temple, we held the ancestor worship ritual, which was similar to the ceremony I remembered from the village, and we honored the Buddha. In the re-education that we had received at the children's home, neither the Buddha nor the prayers or rituals were mentioned, but later on I had managed to read a lot about him and his teachings, and I could relate to them.

Immediately after the ceremony, we sat down with our guests at the long tables of the temple for a meatless meal. I was glad that so many of our friends from the hotel were there, including those that we weren't so close to. The tables were filled, and I was pleased to celebrate our wedding with so many people. At the temple, they explained to me that as part of the ceremony, I had to pour the wine. The monks brought me red cloth, and asked me to wrap it around myself. Though I loved my wedding dress, it was important to me to do everything according to tradition, and so, wrapped in the red fabric, I passed between all the guests and poured more and more wine, until all the bottles were empty.

When the meal was over and everyone was in a good mood,

Shaohan got up on the table and asked all the guests to take the leftover food in boxes, as is customary at weddings in China. We knew that this is what was done at the end of weddings, but our guests were not so keen to take the unseasoned vegetarian food that was served at the temple. Some of Shaohan's friends saw this, and collected the leftovers so that we would not be embarrassed.

Shaohan and I stood at the entrance to the temple and bid farewell to our guests. I felt that the ceremony had passed by too quickly. To this day, I am not sure that I remember exactly everything that happened there.

When we returned to the hotel, to the presidential suite that the manager let us use as his wedding present, a surprise was waiting for us. The mattress that was always covered with fabric and rested on wooden boxes was raised by an additional box spring. On the mattress lay several types of fruits, as the families in our village were accustomed to rest on the newlyweds' bed. The fruit was placed in the form of a large heart that covered the entire bed. There were dates that formed the outline of the heart, and inside it were peanuts and yellow lilac fruits. Around the heart were scattered lotus flower seeds. I was very moved by the sight of the celebratory heart, I liked seeing that someone had taken time to maintain our Chinese tradition for me. But suddenly I felt weak, and fell weeping on the wedding bed.

The night in the luxurious hotel suite was the first night that Shaohan and I were completely alone outside of our home, but it was also the most agonizing night I had with him. I didn't know who to be angry at, at myself, or at him, over the fact that we had married without the presence of our parents. I felt that that evening I had for the first time given up the dream to return to the village, and the entire night I was tormented by disturbing thoughts.

Despite the painful thoughts, that night I also felt great love for Shaohan, for his understanding me and allowing me to agonize, and not trying to divert my thoughts, except for a few words that he also felt a tug at his heart that his parents were missing, but it wasn't so hard for him because he assumed that they would certainly be pleased with his choice. Though our stories were not the same, that evening I appreciated him for what he said, and particularly for what he did not say.

I didn't find lying on the gigantic beautiful bed very comfortable. I fell into it and felt that I was lying on large cold pebbles. Every position was painful; every movement threw me onto another stone. I felt the pain hit me inside more than on my body. I didn't feel stable on the bed. Dizzy or maybe confused, I tried to find a position that didn't hurt. That night there was no such position. I was angry at myself, but the anger wasn't greater than the pain, and the two celebrated my wedding night with me.

Before I closed my eyes, I remembered images and sights from the village of my birth. I tried to distract myself, but the more I tried to do that, the more I failed. I was ashamed that on my wedding night I didn't manage to be a wife to my husband, or even a friend.

Freedom

Ten months from my wedding night I was about to give birth, at the age of 21. The pregnancy had passed like a dream, in the blink of an eye. As my stomach grew, I was able to more effectively push aside thoughts from the past. I was determined to provide warmth to my son or daughter, to give the baby everything that I had been robbed of. Already in the second month, Shaohan had built a cradle, and we decorated the baby's room with pastel-colored paper butterflies.

Nothing that I had been told was anything like what I felt the moment the first wave of pain crashed into me. At first I felt short and unpleasant contractions. I took deep breaths, as Tina had explained to me. I was overcome with excitement, along with deep apprehension of the process to come, and of what would come after it. Several hours passed in anticipation of an increased pace of contractions. When they had increased to an impossible intensity, I was overcome with a paralyzing fear. How was it that I was giving birth to a baby, when I myself still felt like a little girl?

All my attempts to convince myself to breathe deeply and stay relaxed were ground up in the blender that seemed to be pushing against my lower back. I remembered nothing of what I had planned to do. I heard myself breathing like a dog who had just returned from a run in the field. I moved from side to side in the chair, pleading for a few minutes' relief from the pain. And when the few short minutes finally came, I was terrified with the thought that any second the pain would be back, and after it, I would be holding a baby that I would have no idea what to do with. I was alone, without my parents and without my husband. I knew that Shaohan had already left the hotel and he was on his way to bring me to the hospital, but I felt tremendous loneliness sucking me down, down to a place that hurt even more than the contractions. I remembered the stories that my mother would tell me before I went to sleep, especially the story of the monk—my mother didn't remember his name, but knew that he was an important Buddhist monk, and that she had also heard his story from her mother. The monk always sat outside in the country, in the lotus position, and his stories were always fascinating. I had read several meditation training books, and I had tried countless times to sit quietly in front of a view or a wall, but I never lasted very long; my legs ached, and I got very bored.

So I tried again to practice meditation, to not think of anything and to concentrate on my breathing, but the only thing I managed to do well was to grasp the armrest of the chair with all my might, just as I had held onto the observation post in the rice fields on the day that I had tried to escape from the children's home. At some point, neither the pressure on the chair nor the panting were any help, and my attempt to think about other things failed, with each contraction that ground my lower back and tortured me with fierce pains.

I tried to change my position on the chair, but nothing kept me from sinking to the depths of the inhuman pain that I felt. At one point, I remembered the terrible pain I had felt when I was in solitary confinement at the children's home, but I was quick to push away those thoughts from my mind so as not to taint this important day, the day on which life would burst out of me, with memories from the humiliating life at the children's home.

But somehow the image of Anchi's blue body and face in her bed after she froze in the children's home managed to sneak into my mind. I also imagined Deshi, whose panic-stricken face on the night we were taken to the children's home was well-engraved in my memory. To what fate would I be exposing my child? I thought to myself. I tried to overcome the bitter distress I felt, telling myself over and over again that I was now starting a family with Shaohan, and that I would do everything possible so that the lives of our children would be happier than ours had been. And thus, at the time that the memories were causing me distress, the contractions redeemed me from the memory of the pain. The intervals during which I could breathe freely became greatly reduced. I eagerly looked forward to Shaohan's arrival. I told myself that maybe I would wait for him outside the apartment, but I already couldn't carry my body. That was the moment when I understood that the pain caused by labor contractions could not be described in words. I imagined that no woman had ever managed to precisely describe birth, which I had yet to experience. I hoped with all my heart that those horrific pains were only being suffered by me, and that the fetus inside of me did not feel them.

In the few minutes where I managed to breathe properly, after I stopped my breathing in an attempt to overcome the pains climbing my body, I thought about the one-child policy in China, the law that led to my being taken from my parents' home to a cruel life with much suffering. The law allowed every woman to give birth only once. The law, even if passed for justifiable economic reasons, was a cruel law that prevented women from giving birth, people from establishing families, and children from growing up with siblings. This terrible law took my parents from me and robbed me of my childhood.

Again there was a contraction in the form of a knife penetrating to my tailbone, slicing its way up my spine, and cutting through my flesh in a circular motion. My stomach contracted by itself, and I could no longer stand it, and I was afraid that if I lost consciousness it would cause damage to the fetus, and then I heard the door open and Shaohan's steps, and I yelled to him voicelessly, "Help me!"

***

The taxi trip with Shaohan to the hospital did not register in any of my senses. I remembered that we left the apartment, and that I leaned all my weight on him. The only thing I remembered after that was the hospital. Shaohan brought me a wheel chair because I was no longer able to walk. I had the feeling that a giant mass was trying to burst out of me, and I was afraid that if I moved my legs apart, it would pop out of me.

They lay me down on the bed, around me stood nurses, their mouths covered by surgical masks, and I couldn't see whether the expression on their faces was serious, or maybe smiling. I could only hear their voices and the instructions I received. "Don't push yet," I heard one of them tell me. I looked at Shaohan who stood next to me looking pale, as I had never seen him. Shaohan, the strong man who always said the right thing at the right time, had nothing to say. I had the feeling that the contractions attacking me were hurting him too. I remembered with a smile during the first months of the pregnancy, when I suffered from serious nausea, that Shaohan was the one who had vomited.

I gripped his hand during the few seconds that I managed to breath between the contractions. We didn't know if the fetus inside of me was a boy or a girl, and in any case, we had spoken about how we wouldn't stop at just one child, that we wanted more children. But when the terrible knife sliced me again and again, I thought to myself that one child would be quite enough for me, even without the one child law...

A gigantic boulder stood between my legs and wanted to come out. "You're not completely dilated," one of the nurses called, "so try not to push," said another nurse from behind her mask.

"Enough, enough, enough!!!" I screamed for the first time in the hospital. Shaohan was frightened and looked at me helplessly, but the nurses continued doing what they were doing, and didn't even look up when I screamed. It couldn't be that all women giving birth suffered such pain, I thought. Maybe it's only me who had such pain, and I was being punished for something that I had done.

"Are you ready?" the nurse asked and looked at me.

"Ready for what?" I asked in exhaustion.

"Let's go, time to give birth, push!" Those were the liberating words that I said over and over in my head. I gathered all the strength I had lost in the last hours, I breathed deeply and pushed Ziyou out. The baby that I had chosen to call "Freedom" was about to enter the world. "Wait, the head came out." I heard one of the nurses. "Hold on, we'll help you." All at once I felt that the fetus that was inside of me flowed out, and with it a warm wave that had been the contents of my womb that had enveloped it for nine months.

"It's a girl," the nurse announced, holding a small living being wrapped in a blanket. Shaohan started to sob and didn't know whether to look at the baby or me. Suddenly there was a loud wail, and I immediately started crying and joined in. In all the excitement, I hadn't noticed that the pains had subsided. Later on, I understood that soon after the birth, the pain and its intensity are erased from our memory, and the happiness that comes with the birth compensates for all the pain.

I would like to describe clearly the pain that I felt, so that other women would be able to get some idea of it. But maybe it isn't possible to really describe that pain, and from this stems the women's code of silence. Because if women knew what the pain was really like, they wouldn't give birth, if they knew of the difficulty involved in raising babies, of the concern that comes with raising children, of the worry involved in dealing with teenagers, it's possible that they wouldn't have very many children. Apparently this code of silence stems from the desire of women to give birth without taking into account the pain, the fears, the worries or the other difficulties. I think of the silence of the women over the years that I raised my daughter, the years that she kept me busy and worried me boundlessly, I think of their silence, and I keep silent too.

After the birth I was completely exhausted, but Shaohan was restless, spoke constantly, and was not able to leave the room or me. Since I wanted him to go, I managed to convince him to go to the hotel to tell everyone that he was the father of a little girl. After he left, I didn't manage to fall asleep, despite the exhaustion, but I was happy to be alone and think about the charge that had descended on me the moment that I heard the cry of our Ziyou.

A Raging River

We went home with Ziyou. I asked Shaohan to hold her so that I could take a shower, but he was afraid and asked that I wait until she had fallen asleep. I sat on the only comfortable chair that we had in the apartment, and held her in the nursing position that the nurse had taught me in the hospital. Ziyou opened her mouth, put it around my nipple, and started to suck. Every time she sucked she made noises, possibly from enjoyment or in her efforts to suck. Shaohan looked at us and laughed, and I, who was still in pain, asked him to stop so that he wouldn't disturb her. Ziyou's beautiful eyes closed and her sucking became less intense, until I felt that she had fallen asleep. I put her in the middle of our bed, covered her with a blanket, and left Shaohan to watch over her breathing.

I rinsed my seemingly deformed body in warm water, stroked my empty but still swollen stomach. I looked at my chest that had become much larger, pressed my breasts and watched the milk stream from them, the milk with which I would nourish my daughter. I saw that I was still bleeding, but remembered what the nurse had told me and understood that that was okay. I knew nothing else about anything, because neither my mother nor any other woman was with me to help.

Evening fell and Ziyou woke up from her long nap straight

into my arms. Shaohan had already left for the evening shift at work, and for the moment I was so happy that I didn't know what to do with myself. Ziyou started to move restlessly in my arms and whimpered softly. I offered her my breast, but after a few sucks, she began to cry and moved her mouth away.

I stood up and started to move around the apartment so that she would relax, but that didn't help. The crying turned into a roar, as if she was in pain. I rocked her in my arms and tried to find a position that would calm her, but to no avail, and in the meantime, my body started to hurt.

I kept trying to feed her, but the crying did not allow it. I tried to lie her down in bed alone, I tried to hug her tightly, I tried to caress her gently, I tried to walk quickly around the apartment, but nothing helped. Finally, despite my efforts not to, I started to cry more loudly than she was. It seemed as though she was surprised by my crying, but that was just for a moment because after that, cries erupted from her mouth which I was able to hear between my cries.

I undressed her to find out if she had a bruise or scratch anywhere, but this only made her scream harder. Through all this crying, I tried to sing her the song my mother had sung to me as a child, but my desperate singing didn't calm her.

I decided to try to wash her, so I took off my own clothes, held her tightly so she wouldn't slide from my arms, and we got into the shower together. The water was cold at first but gradually it warmed up, and in the meantime we were awash in my tears, whose flow had increased with my desperation. When the water was warm enough, we both got into the shower and the crying stopped; the flowing water on her body seemed to surprise her. I hugged her little body and we stood together under the shower for a long time. I felt that I was about to faint, but I still managed to find the strength to hold her, and I knew that I would be able to hold her as long as necessary. The longing for my mother returned, just like during the first days in the children's home, longing that hurt and that caused heavy aches in the chest, yearning that ended in bitter weeping.

Suddenly, I heard Ziyou's weeping. She started to cry because she had gotten used to the stream of water. I closed my eyes, and the water that washed our bodies sent me back to my little house in the village. My mother had wrapped us in a large piece of colorful fabric. She smiled at us, and Ziyou stopped crying. I opened my eyes and looked at my wet baby, and I promised myself that I would never ever leave her.

I shut the faucet and reached for a towel. I wrapped us both in it and gently wiped dry my daughter's perfect little body. I lay her down on the bed, and she seemed to me such a tiny helpless creature, but she was mine. The skin of her little feet was wrinkled from having been in water for so long. Her tiny feet reminded me of the feet of one of our neighbors in the village. Though the custom of tying feet to keep them small was no longer observed when I was born, there were still some mothers who tied the feet of their daughters so they would be privileged to married an honorable man. I remember that my girlfriends and I would take a peek at the twisted feet of the neighbor and become totally disgusted at the sight. Not only were they small, they also looked like a curled up animal, the toes folded under the sole, and this was apparently the reason that our neighbor barely left the house and found it difficult to walk. For a moment I smiled when I thought of her, and wondered who the honorable man was that she had ultimately married.

I caressed Ziyou's body wrapped in the towel and noticed that she had calmed down and closed her eyes. Maybe the many hours that she had cried had exhausted her and therefore she had fallen asleep. The next thing I felt was Shaohan covering me, and I understood that I had fallen asleep naked next to her.

***

I awoke to the sound of Ziyou's crying, and I started to cry again too. But now Shaohan was there with me. He got up from the blanket spread out on the floor on which he had fallen asleep, and asked, "What happened?" I told him that Ziyou had cried the entire evening and that I hadn't known what to do. Shaohan, who saw how I felt but he himself also didn't know what to do with a crying baby, said that in the morning he would ask one of the neighbors in the building to explain to us what to do.

At first I objected, because I was ashamed that I was incapable of being a mother. How could I be a mother if my mother had been stolen from me? Ziyou's crying angered me. I didn't feel what I was supposed to feel: compassion, tenderness, softness. Trapped inside my own chest was the scream of an orphan baby, the cry of a little lost girl – me. I wanted hugs and caresses. I wanted to scream, but I couldn't. I was tired to death, wrung out like laundry now being hung on the line. All I wanted to do was to sleep while being hugged and caressed, to take and take endlessly, and not to give a thing. It was hard for me to feel that I wasn't capable of taking care of a baby. I was also afraid that Shaohan would think that I wasn't mature enough to be a mother. But after a night of no sleep and much crying, I agreed to his suggestion. I surrendered to my exhaustion, and it would appear that Shaohan had already learned to hear me even if I didn't speak.

When the sun came up, Ziyou fell asleep for a few hours. I didn't know that that would be a long sleep, and I continued to watch her, afraid that she would wake up. I looked at her fine little face that looked so angelic when she slept. Her head was covered with soft black down, and her nose was so small that I didn't understand how she could even breathe. I looked at this wonder that had come from my body, and I knew that my life had changed. I understood that until that point I had taken care of myself, and had done everything I needed in order to survive, but that from then on I needed to take care of my daughter first. All at once I understood that I had to change, to know how to give and not only to take. The thoughts of my nights in the village tormented me, but I swore to myself and to her that she would not be a child of the night, and that no one would ever take her from me.

I hoped that my baby would stop crying so much after a few months, when she managed to digest my milk. The thought passed through my mind that there was something in me and my milk that was bad for her, but I knew that I was doing the right thing, and continued to nurse her. The first days passed relatively quietly, and I stayed in bed most of the time. The nights, on the other hand, were sleepless. I didn't manage to calm Ziyou down, and her crying never stopped.

The baby and taking care of her were the only things that interested me during the first month of her life. Whenever she cried, I cried uncontrollably along with her. When she finally fell asleep, I found myself sitting and crying for no apparent reason. The happiness that had filled me right after the birth had disappeared, leaving emptiness inside of me. I was angry at myself for my helplessness, for my inability to be happy, and the anger made me weepy and exhausted.

Shaohan was very patient with both the baby and me. When he was home, he did everything to make it easier for me, but he still refused to hold the baby in his arms. "She is so small," he said fearfully, "I am afraid to drop her. Let's wait until she grows a bit." And I in my fatigue accepted his words.

***

One evening, Shaohan returned from the morning shift with one of the neighbors, the one that always gave me a friendly hello when we met on the stairs. She introduced herself by her Western name, Lily, and said that she had heard from Shaohan that it was difficult for me to take care of the baby. Her words were like a slap in the face. I became very angry at Shaohan that he didn't believe in my skills as a mother and was looking for women to help me. I locked myself in the bathroom.

I sat on the toilet and waited for the tears and loud sobs that I had known for many days, but instead of tears, anger flowed, anger that seemed like a raging muddy river. A river that normally flowed peacefully, with clear water, but this time it was full of tears, crashing against the boulders, trying to burst beyond its banks. I wasn't afraid to swim in this river, on the contrary, suddenly I wanted to jump into it and have the water sweep me away. I had already been thrown into rivers and survived. My mother had never come to save me during all those years, and also now that I had given birth, there was no one to help me understand how to take care of this little being that had come from me.

And why should my mother come now and help me? I thought in rage. All those years she hadn't come to take me home, hadn't tried to reach into the stormy water to help me get out. And I had swum alone, had fought alone, and survived without her. And now I didn't need her help. What help could she give me with my daughter, when she hadn't managed to help her one and only daughter?

The river continued to storm around me, and the dragon inside of me began to move toward it, to provoke the rushing water, to shoot fire at the river, to move at the pace the water flowed. A multicolored dragon of sharp colors—red, orange, purple, and green—on the background of the dull brown river. My anger turned very dark and cruel—I would never forgive my mother for seeing me battle with the river and not trying to take me out of it, I decided. How could she have been so cruel with such a young girl? How could it be that she hadn't found me all those years? All the years that I yearned for her so and believed that she would come to take me home were one big illusion. She hadn't even tried to look for me, she probably just gave up on me that very night. I didn't need help from such a mother, I told myself, and I certainly wouldn't be like her.

When I heard Ziyou crying, I hurried out of the bathroom to tend to her. Shaohan and Lily were still waiting for me near our bed. I picked up the baby from the bed and sat on the chair to nurse her. Lily stood next to me and stroked my hair. I tried to ignore her and continue with what I was supposed to be doing. "What's happening to you, and what you are experiencing, happens to every woman after birth," Lily started to explain in the tone of a classroom teacher. "The flood of hormones in your body causes your uncontrollable crying and emotional turmoil." Lily kneeled down next to me and tried to catch my eye. "You are no different from anyone else who has given birth," she said quietly. "And as far as I can see, you are doing well." That time I looked her in the eye and listened.

"Your baby is suffering from intestinal cramps and digestive problems, all of which are very common in newborn babies. These problems disappear in a few months." Ziyou continued nursing, and I gradually calmed down and noticed that what she was saying was the same as what the first neighbor who had visited us had said. I looked at her and she continued explaining, "What you are feeling will also disappear in time, but it is definitely possible for you to start feeling better already. You have to eat properly, leave the house for a walk with the baby, and you must sleep." I smiled at her gratefully, and she returned the smile.

When Ziyou finished nursing, Lily reached over to me and asked to hold her. Very gently, I passed the baby to her, and hugging the baby, she turned to Shaohan, "You must start helping Ming," she said gently, "and you must make sure that she sleeps well and gets stronger." Shaohan approached her hesitantly and put out his hands to take the baby. Lily put Ziyou in his arms and showed him how to support her head so that it wouldn't fall backwards. Shaohan hugged his daughter with great emotion and began to stutter, "This… is this okay?" he asked, and Lily and I both laughed at the sight of the trembling man standing before us. My anger at Shaohan faded with the laugh that washed over me.

Good kind Lily remained with us the entire evening, and thanks to her devoted care, I realized how much I missed my mother, and how much I wanted to return to the village.

Identity Card 20

The brown envelope with Ziyou's birth certificate arrived two weeks after the birth. When I took out this certificate, I immediately understood that it was my chance to travel to visit my mother and father. Everything ran quickly through my head, and I forgot completely how angry I was with my mother.

I knew what I had to do, but I was afraid of Shaohan's reaction. I already knew what he thought of my wish to travel to the village from our discussion before the wedding, but I couldn't ignore the fact that my daughter's birth certificate was my ticket to China and back. It didn't even occur to me to suggest that he join me on the visit. I knew that it was impossible for us both to take off from work at the hotel, and I figured that he wouldn't be interested. Was I embarrassed, deep down, to introduce him to my parents?

As if possessed, I quickly wrapped Ziyou in her orange blanket, and tied her onto my body in the baby carrier to take her out of the house. I didn't want to take her on the crowded train, so I had to take three buses to reach the Interior Ministry. The line at the ministry was very long, and in the meantime I sat and filled out forms. For the first time, I registered my true Chinese name and origin without fear, because I knew that since my daughter had been born in Hong Kong,

I was also entitled to a certificate of citizenship and not just a residence permit.

Surprisingly, I was not at all afraid of submitting papers with the authorities. Apparently the little baby I had tied onto myself gave me the strength to believe that this was the right thing to do. For a moment, I had no regret that I was doing all this without Shaohan's approval, in fact, without his knowledge. I planned to tell him, I rationalized to myself, but the envelope arrived after he had left for work.

I quickly filled out the form, and when Ziyou woke up, I took her to the women's restroom to nurse her, away from the prying eyes of the people all around. When I returned, I found out that the line had barely moved, and I started to lose patience. I asked the official at the entrance why it took so long. When I heard his answer, I understood for the first time that people perceived me as a mother.

I still didn't feel like a mother on the outside, I didn't think that people could see that I was a mother, and I didn't connect between the baby on me and the title, until I heard the official speak: "With a baby, you don't wait in line." I already knew from reading books how happy one sentence could make someone, but this time, the sentence both made me happy that it cut down my waiting time, and gave me such satisfaction that I got something because of my new status as a mother.

"Lady, go to the clerk on the left, she will take you ahead of the line," the official said. The good feeling that spread throughout my body led me to the clerk without fear. For a moment, I didn't think about what would happen if they understood that I only had a residence permit, and was not a citizen of Hong Kong, and decided to deport me. Only when I was on the way home on the bus, crying with excitement, and at the same time, fear of going home, only then did I think of the danger that I might have taken upon myself, and hadn't looked into very deeply.

When I got home, I quickly prepared Shaohan's favorite soup. I straightened up the house, nursed Ziyou again, and then washed her to remove all the smells she had absorbed outside. I walked around the house restlessly, and kept looking for some way to occupy myself until Shaohan came home.

Shaohan had already had several furious outbursts in the past. He had become angry several times when I wanted to go to the library frequently instead of being with him. He had given me the silent treatment every time I mentioned how much I wanted to return to China and see my parents. Now, I was afraid that he would explode with all the anger that he had built up when I revealed my plans to travel home, to China, with our daughter. Though it was clear to me that it was only a visit, my heart pounded so hard that I imagined that Ziyou could feel it and therefore moved uneasily in her little bed. I looked at her and my eyes filled with tears. What kind of world had I brought her into? What kind of world had I brought myself to? I was again a victim, a leaf blown by the wind.

Shaohan came home smiling as usual, and before he had had a chance to take off his jacket, I announced, "Ziyou and I have citizenship papers, and we are going to visit my parents."

After that sentence had been thrown into the air, I found myself in a foreign place. Shaohan didn't let me continue speaking. His face reddened with anger, and his fists were so tight that they also became red, ready to explode like two grenades in his hands.

"Listen a minute," I tried to calm him, "it's only for a few days…"

"Don't you dare leave the apartment," his face was red, and his eyes seemed to pop out of place when he screamed at me.

"You lied to me, you married me and had a baby just so you could return to China," he yelled. The words came out of his mouth like from a machine gun pointed directly at my head. His neck swelled and reddened, and spittle sprayed from his mouth as he screamed.

There was no compassion in his voice when he screamed at me. My heart pounded, my body froze. He continued to scream, and suddenly he grabbed my shoulders forcefully, shook me, and sat me down on the chair. I covered my face with my hands to protect myself, cried and begged him, "Stop please, you are hurting me."

I had fallen again into the dark, cold room in the children's home. I was pushed to the lowest place I had known, a place that I so hadn't want to return to. My fragile body that still hadn't recovered from birth was shrinking back in an attempt to protect itself.

But he continued to kick everything in the room, fortunately only objects. "Liar, liar, liar," he yelled at me with each kick, at an increasing pace.

I didn't dare turn my face toward him or look at him. I remembered the week when I was punished for my attempt to escape from the children's home, when I suffered from pain so strong that I felt nothing else. I let out screams of pain without his registering them. Suddenly, I remembered that my daughter could hear me, and I immediately lowered my voice. I felt devoid of life and completely threatened. I huddled on the floor and saw the table turn over next to me, and after it the chairs crashed to the floor. After that, Shaohan flung everything that he managed to grab in the kitchen. The objects didn't hit me, but crashed next to me. For a time, I was concentrating entirely on not getting hurt, but in a moment of respite, I understood that I had to get up to protect Ziyou. I sprang up from the floor all at once, while avoiding Shaohan. I lay down next to her on the little mattress I had placed on the floor next to our bed. I sheltered her with my body.

Shaohan approached and tried to move me away from her. "Don't you dare touch her! Don't you dare take her!" he screamed again and again. I held my baby tightly, and tried in vain to keep myself from crying. Ziyou woke up from the cries and screams, and she too started crying. Her crying caused Shaohan to stop screaming immediately, and I took advantage of this; on trembling legs, I stood up and held her against me. I looked at Shaohan and his angry red face and raging eyes, and with my eyes pleaded that he not hurt us. I tried to feed Ziyou to calm her, but she refused to suckle and just cried in pain. Shaohan stopped his violent tantrum for a moment, looked at her with concern, and started to approach us. I turned my back on him and shielded Ziyou from her father. His violence had surprised me and caught me off guard.

With my back to him, I sensed that Shaohan was approaching with slow steps, but his breathing was still rapid. He wrapped his arms around me, and I shrank away in such a way so as not to crush the baby but still protect her. I was still afraid that he would hurt us, but his hug didn't hurt. He put his hands on me gently, and only when he said, "Excuse me, I'm sorry," did I understand that he was trying to hug me. But I didn't trust him not to attack me again, and I didn't want him to touch me, so I shook him off without saying a word. I took advantage of the lull and walked from place to place around the room in an effort to calm Ziyou.

Shaohan moved away from me and started to straighten up the room. He picked up the table and chairs, which stood askew, and with slow movements, picked up all the kitchen utensils that he had thrown to the floor. Ziyou relaxed in my arms and fell asleep exhausted by her crying, and only then did I hear Shaohan's weeping—the loudest crying I had ever heard.

I returned Ziyou to the mattress and lay down next to her, catching my breath and remembering that here in Hong Kong I had rights. No one could hurt me or limit my movements. I grew up in a place where the regime had taken away my freedom and did with me as it wished. Fate had led me to my freedom, and though Shaohan was the one who had helped me, he had no right to take it away from me. These thoughts encouraged and strengthened me. I remained lying on the floor and apparently fell asleep, because when I woke up, the house was dark, and Shaohan was sleeping on the bed. I glanced around the room and saw that Shaohan had straightened it up as best as he could.

I looked at my husband sleeping in his clothes on our bed, and I felt that I was living with a strange man. Maybe I did something to hurt him, but I had not expected such a violent tantrum as that. I lay awake and vigilant for the morning ahead.

Ziyou started to move in her sleep and woke up to the familiar quiet. When she opened her eyes I looked at her, and resolved that I would never let anyone hurt her, certainly not someone who was supposed to protect her. This promise raised once again the image of my mother being pushed by the police officer and falling on the ground when the truck that took me away began to drive. I resolved that I would do everything necessary so that Ziyou would not have such images in her memory.

Baby Formula

Shaohan was facing me when he opened his eyes. I was sitting on the floor nursing Ziyou. He was looking at me but hadn't yet lifted his head from the pillow. I looked into his eyes and tried to understand who he really was. I took a deep breath so as not to further stress my baby.

I had always believed in fate. Sometimes it had shaken me and thrown me to a new and difficult life, and sometimes it had extended its hand to release me from a life of suffering, and opened a door to something good that was to happen to me. In my life, there had been many jolts and also many doors opening that had led me to a better path. It had been easy to accept things in the faith that that was my fate, that I had no control over it. It was only a question of living with what had been given to me and trying to understand it. My life was like a story I had read about someone else, and except for my failed attempt to escape from the children's home, I actually had not decided a thing, and had done nothing to change my fate.

I almost never gave any thought to my fate or my life, because I had been drowning in a battle for survival, flooded with longing. My obtaining the citizenship in Hong Kong was apparently another attempt to create a different fate for myself, one that would have me reunite with my parents, but also allow me to return to Shaohan. The man lying in front of me, watching me nurse the baby, seemed so foreign to me that I could even think for a moment that it was really him.

I had returned to a bad place like on the day they took me from my parents. At this point, if I wanted to return to them, it was my partner who was preventing me from doing so. I moved Ziyou to the other breast, and took another deep breath to overcome the pressure that was incapacitating me. From the time we met, Shaohan had always wrapped me in his confidence, reassured me, supported me, and was my friend. If anyone had told me that he would be violent or scream at me, I would have just laughed. Maybe my young age and lack of experience wasn't helping me read his behavior during our fights. Was it that I didn't want to believe it? Or that I didn't really see in him features that indicated that he could be violent? I thought about this as I nursed Ziyou. I knew that I had no choice but to speak with him, with the stranger lying in front of me, or I would need to run away from him.

Shaohan looked at me for a long time, and without picking up his head said, "I'm sorry that I frightened you."

I stayed still so that the baby would continue nursing, but I was afraid. I didn't trust Shaohan's plea for forgiveness, but I wanted to put it all behind me, as if nothing had happened, as if the furniture was standing in its place and wasn't strewn all over. I continued to sit quietly, because I didn't know what to say.

Shaohan lowered his eyes from me in the hopes that I would answer, but I decided not to respond. He lay motionless in bed, and continued looking at me. Every once in a while he would mumble, "I'm sorry." He did not get up for work, and I continued to take care of the baby to maintain her daily routine.

About 15 minutes passed that seemed like an eternity. I put Ziyou on my shoulder, and stroked her back hard so that she would burp or even spit up, and as I was stroking her, I felt a pain in the shoulder she was resting on. The fear that Shaohan would rise and explode again did not leave me, but I tried not to show it to Ziyou. I laid her back down on the mattress next to me and leaned on the wall, preparing my answer for the man that I felt I no longer knew, after what had happened last night.

"I don't know you," I began quietly. "You, who picked me up and took care of me, suddenly throw furniture around violently in front of our baby, and yell at me until I have no idea who you are."

"You're right," Shaohan said and rose a little. "I don't... I also don't know what got into me."

"It doesn't help me very much to be right at this point," I said angrily.

"I meant that you were right when you said that I was wrong." He was quiet for a moment, and then looked straight at me and said, "You also dealt me a blow."

"A blow? But I didn't even touch you!" I answered assertively, though I was careful not to raise my voice so as not to frighten Ziyou.

"I meant what you told me," he also answered without raising his voice, and sat up straight.

"There is still no justification for what you did to us, to me and your daughter."

"I would never hurt either of you in any way!" he raised his voice.

"You already hurt her!" I answered. "Because she saw and heard you yesterday. To scream at me, to fling things that could hurt me – that also hurt her." I spoke quickly and firmly because I didn't want him to present the incident differently from what I had experienced.

"Enough, please, don't cause me to jump out the window. You don't understand that I was afraid of losing you!" Shaohan's voice was anguished, but despite my surprise, I remained suspicious. Was he trying to divert the conversation, or did he want to frighten me in another way?

"Yes, but now, after what you did, you really have lost me." Suddenly I couldn't look at him, I didn't want to have compassion for him, I was still so angry.

"I beg you," he spoke more quietly. "Forgive me, please." Shaohan put his hands together in supplication, or maybe it was a sign of prayer.

"If I forgive you this time, how do I know that it won't happen again?" I said in a confident voice to strengthen my argument.

"I thought that you were running away from me with the baby," he said and lowered his eyes, and didn't look up even when Ziyou started to move uncomfortably and make noises in protest.

"But I never meant to run away!" I shouted angrily. "I wanted to travel to visit my parents and return. I waited for this moment for so many years, and I finally have an opportunity to visit them. Not for a moment did I think not to return," I added and tears welled in my eyes.

"But you didn't say that," said Shaohan with a broken voice, still looking at the floor.

"Because you didn't let me explain!" I said in protest, trying to find a position that Ziyou would be comfortable in. "You shrieked at me, threw the entire contents of the house near me—how could I explain anything?"

"I didn't understand..." he answered quietly. But then he regained his composure and shouted, "And why did you apply for the certificate without telling me? That was why I thought you were running away." Instead of supplications, there was restrained anger in his voice.

I wanted to understand him, but I held my ground. "So it's too bad that I didn't run away," I said stubbornly. "Then I wouldn't have found out that my husband was a violent person." Instead of looking at him, I took care of the baby. I rocked her in my arms, lay her down on her stomach, and stroked her back.

"You're right," said Shaohan and tried to change the tone of the conversation. "But I still would have traveled there to bring you back."

Ziyou continued to move uncomfortably, and for a moment we both looked at her quietly, at the little girl that connected us to each other. I picked her up and hugged her again. I still hadn't looked in the mirror to see my face which hurt from my endless crying.

I asked Shaohan if he was planning to go to work.

"No," he answered. "I can't, I don't want to leave you two. I'm really very sorry." He leaned his back on the wall and looked at me.

"What, are you afraid that I'll run away?" I objected. "In any case, I'm going to travel to my parents. Whether I return or not – after what has happened, I'll have to think seriously about that."

My words caused Shaohan to move away from the wall and move toward me, still sitting up in bed. For a second I was afraid that the violence would return, but he covered his face with his hands and started to cry.

I had no feeling of victory or desire for revenge, I really felt sorry for him. I understood his fear that we would travel and not return, and I also understood his fear of desertion, but I was still angry.

"I'm not running away, and I never planned to run away," I said quietly. "That's why I told you that I had obtained the papers. I only want to visit my parents and then return, that's why I applied for Hong Kong citizenship."

"And what if they don't let you return," asked Shaohan, wiping his tears. "What if they find out that the parents of the baby fled China and they arrest you? Do you remember what happened to Chan, who went to his cousin's wedding and was arrested?" he continued firmly. "Not only did he not come back, he was sent to a work camp and has been there for six months."

"I have read many books in the library on citizens' rights, and I checked at the Interior Ministry," I answered, ignoring the story of his friend, "now I am a citizen of Hong Kong, and I have every right to return here."

"I don't know…" Shaohan said, sounding doubtful. "I only know that neither one of us wants to return to China."

"I, as opposed to you, did not leave my family, and I did not receive their blessing," I said angrily. "I was taken from my parents by force, and I must return to them to tell them that I got married and show them Ziyou." I put her on the mattress again, trying to put her to sleep.

"I beg you!" Shaohan raised his voice for the first time in our discussion, but immediately calmed down and continued more quietly. "Don't take Ziyou to China, please, I beg you…"

"What are you afraid of?" I asked him in wonder. "Are you afraid we'll stay there?"

"Maybe," he answered. "Maybe you'll want to stay in the village with your parents and raise her there…"

"After what I went through in China, it never even occurred to me to raise her in that place," I said indignantly, though for a moment I had a thought that maybe I would want to raise her in my mother's house, so that she could help me and ease the great burden.

"So leave her with me, and we'll wait for you here," said Shaohan, as if he'd heard my thoughts.

Tears still glistened in Shaohan's eyes, and his face was red and wet. I could see his pain and fear that we wouldn't return.

"How can I leave her here? I am nursing her and you are working," I answered him after considering what he had said.

"I don't know… so just don't go, please."

"You forget that yesterday you tried to destroy our entire home," returning to my argument in a desperate attempt not to lose the argument.

"That wasn't me," said Shaohan in a hoarse voice, and I could see how he was trying with all his might to prevent the sobs from bursting out. "A demon entered me and did what he wanted, and I tell you again how ashamed and sorry I am. I promise you that that won't happen again." It sounded as if with that he was winding up our discussion.

"I would really like to believe you…" I said, and I really wanted to.

There was silence, and I took advantage of the break in the discussion to dress Ziyou. "I am going to take Ziyou out for a little walk," I said.

"Fine" Shaohan said, and got up from the bed. His voice sounded more hopeful. "I'll wait for you two here; I'm going to take a shower. I hope you come back," he added quietly. When

I didn't answer, he said, "Maybe you should wash your face before you go out."

"I prefer not to see myself right now," I answered in a serious tone.

"Should I bring you a towel?"

"Don't bring me anything, and leave me alone," I said firmly.

"I want you to return and forgive me," he said, and headed for the bathroom.

"I never meant not to return," I said, already tired of repeating things over and over. "You expect me to forgive you, but you don't believe me."

"Fine, okay, I'll be quiet. The things I'm saying are not coming out the way I want them to." He looked at me and in a quiet voice said, "I love you and I want you to stay with me."

In the meantime, Ziyou fell asleep, and I packed the baby bag, changed my clothes, and was ready to go out. Shaohan stood and watched us. I saw the worry in his eyes, but I knew that for the time being, I was going to return.

***

I went out and stood on the street with Ziyou, trying to decide where to go. Though the air was thick and sooty, I didn't want to stay home, and wanted Ziyou to be out awhile and I wanted to recover from what had happened and think quietly about my travel plans. I noticed the looks I was getting in the street, and at first thought that people were just looking at a young girl carrying her baby, but since I had already been outside with her and no one had paid any attention to us, I figured that they were looking at me since they saw signs of my apprehension.

For hours I walked around between the buildings, entering

pretty gardens hidden between the skyscrapers, and I tried not to feel the loneliness that was hanging over me. I felt like a little grain against the power of the giant buildings in Hong Kong. I wanted to feel my power as a resident of the city, but felt that I didn't belong there. I wanted to feel that I belonged, and the scent of my mother returned and stabbed me sharply, along with the sight of the fields from my childhood village in spring.

Groups of people practicing Tai Chi were a very calming sight. I sat on the bench in the corner of one of the gardens and watched the slow, gentle, flowing movements of the participants. If it weren't for Ziyou being tied to me, I would have stood and let my body sail with them. I thought of my friend Seyoung and was sorry that she wasn't there to consult with. I thought about how I didn't have any true girlfriends in Hong Kong, only Shaohan, and I didn't have anyone to go to. I felt the heaviness join the feeling of pain inside, and the loneliness making me feel empty. For a moment I longed for the way we had slept all together at the children's home, and my friends there, but that thought disturbed me and I quickly put it out of my head.

I decided to go to the library, thinking that maybe the librarian would agree to listen to me for a while. She was smart and was always reading books, I thought, and maybe she had read a similar story and could tell me how it ended. She knew me well just from the books I read. She helped me understand how my life had been formed, and more than anything – why it had turned out that way. She revealed to me what I hadn't known, regarding the regime in China and the re-education program there, which had taken me from my parents to a cruel place. The librarian always smiled, maybe she would show me the right way, maybe she would just listen to me, or give me a consoling hug. These thoughts brought a smile to my lips. I hugged Ziyou and got up to go.

***

I took the bus to the library. I had never been there in the morning, and I hoped that the smiling librarian would be there. Ziyou apparently enjoyed the ride, because she fell asleep on me the minute the bus started to drive. Interesting what Shaohan would think, I thought to myself, when the hours had passed and he saw that we hadn't yet returned, but I had decided not to worry my brain over pity for him. At that moment, I told myself that I would let no one rob me of the freedom that I had obtained. After all I had gone through without having understood what was guiding my fate and my life, I wouldn't let anyone control me. My mother's terrified run and fall as a result of the blow she had received from the police officer were the last memories that I had to allow me to believe that my parents had not cooperated with the authorities; they did not hand me over willingly to the authorities; they did not hand me over willingly for the purpose of re-education, rather they had lost me as a result of an aggressive and violent action. During all those years I had lived in hope that they hadn't given up on me, and therefore I had decided not to give up on myself, certainly not now, a moment before my dream seemed to be coming true. I felt my passion growing each minute to visit my parents and tell them that the party hadn't managed to break me, that I had made it, that fate had given me the freedom to choose for myself, and had led me to a new life as a mother. I wanted to see my mother hug her granddaughter.

Smile her smile at her. Prepare soup for her, tell her the fairy tales that she had told me. I also wanted to see my father, sit her on the seat of the wagon that the neighbor Dewei-Hu had built for the Changs and me when we were very little. I also wanted Ziyou to smell them, to get to know the warmth of their bodies, to cuddle with them and fall asleep in their bed like I used to. I wanted my parents to help me. To continue to raise me.

Much to my surprise, the library was empty. I was embarrassed to ask where the librarian was, whose name I didn't know at all. I stood by the desk, across from the older librarian with the slight mustache. When I saw her for the first time, I had made efforts not to burst out laughing, but since then I had already gotten used to the way she looked. She spoke in a high voice, a little squeaky, and every time that I stood in front of her, I wanted to answer her in a similar voice, but I controlled myself. Her reading glasses, gigantic and black, seemed like very old binocular lenses that she had apparently inherited from her grandfather. She apparently also inherited the mustache from him. I told her that if the baby disturbed people I would leave immediately, but now she was sleeping, and I was looking for a particular book.

The librarian looked at me kindly, and with a quieter voice than usual asked, "Is everything okay?"

"Yes, of course," I answered, surprised at the question, and wondering if she knew something about me. "Why do you ask?" I added.

"Your eyes are so red," she said, and in her voice I heard worry that made me a little afraid.

"Ah, that's nothing, I'm fine," I said, and smiled a big smile to hide my embarrassment. The librarian let it drop and went back to her work.

For the first time in my life I was entering the library carrying a little baby, and the first thing I thought of was how I would teach her to read. I looked around again as if I had entered the library for the first time. I was afraid that in my excitement I would start to tremble, and the trembling would wake up Ziyou. I held my breath to calm down, and imagined how I would sit with Ziyou at home or in the library, and we would read together.

I continued to look at the large hall and the bookcases, and when I turned to the back, I saw my smiling librarian returning books from the cart to the shelves. I approached her silently, stood next to her without saying anything, and waited for her to finish. But she noticed me, smiled at me, and asked me, "Is everything okay?" I figured that she also saw in my face that something bad had happened, but this time I was ready, "Yes, of course, everything is fine. I'll just wash my face, it's really nothing." I hoped that would be sufficient.

"Is the baby yours?" she asked with a smile and peeked at Ziyou.

I smiled back. "The baby's name is Ziyou, and yes, she's my daughter." This was the first time I had introduced her, and I was very moved by that. After that, I became serious, and said to the librarian in a quiet voice, "I'd like to ask a moment of your time."

"With pleasure," she answered.

"Could we sit for a minute?" I asked hopefully. "It's a long story."

"Certainly," she answered. "Have a seat, and I'll join you very soon."

I chose the most distant table and sat in the corner. I was

glad that Ziyou was still sleeping—I didn't want her to hear our conversation; I didn't know what she would understand or take in.

The librarian came back after a few minutes and sat down across from me. It was difficult for me to start talking about myself and my life. I would have preferred to talk about some book or ask a general question, but I knew that I had to get right to the point so as not to bother her at work. "I have no one to consult with on a very important matter." I started and said, "I wanted to get your advice, as someone who is very knowledgeable." I looked down uneasily, and added quietly, "Thank you."

"I'll do anything I can to help you," the librarian answered, and moved her chair closer to me. It took me some time until I started to tell her my whole life's story. I didn't know where to start, and I was also afraid that I would waste the time she had for me, and she would go back to arranging the books. I introduced myself and my origins, even though she probably already knew about all that from the books I had chosen to read, and then gradually continued.

I wasn't precise with all the facts, and I didn't tell her all the details. I told her about the sun that scorched us when we worked in the fields in the summer, about the cold that penetrated every bone in my body when I stood barefoot in the frozen water of the rice fields, about the rations of food, the odor in the children's home that emanated from the bodies of children who hadn't washed or changed their clothes.

I wanted to get to the point at which I could ask her advice on whether to travel back to the village where I was born. There were points in my story where she put out her hand, maybe to try to comfort me—the warmth of her hand on mine was pleasant, maybe it kept me from bursting out in tears. It wasn't often in my life that I had experienced a warm and comforting touch. I felt as if her hand warmed my entire body; I could even imagine that it was my mother's hand.

I couldn't seem to hide my tears or my trembling, though I told her very little of what I had gone through in my short life. Then suddenly I became determined to tell the entire story. I told her how they had kidnapped me, how I had waited for years for my parents to come take me home, how reading was a comfort to me. I told her of my escape attempt, the whistling of the leather strap in my ears, of the letters I had written that apparently hadn't gotten anywhere, and when I got to the escape to Hong Kong, I started speaking at a slower, measured pace. I spared her the stories about Shaohan's angry tantrums, and didn't tell her about the notebook in which I started to write my story.

"And now I would like to travel to the village with Ziyou to visit my parents, and my husband Shaohan objects to this." I looked at her in the expectation that she would solve this dilemma, the question of questions. The librarian smiled her pleasant smile as always. "I understand him," she said. "I know many Chinese people who are afraid to return out of fear that they will be arrested. I also know Chinese people who did travel and did not return. Unfortunately, they are many."

"Yes," I agreed with her. "I also know someone at work that returned to China and was arrested. The regime there is terrible and cruel," I added, "but I feel that I must return to my parents, I must see them, tell them what happened to me, show them their granddaughter…"

"I also understand you," the librarian said. "If I were in your place, I too would want to return to visit my parents.

In any case, it is your decision to make, not your husband's." I listened carefully to every word that she said, expecting to hear full support for my decision, but then she added, "Just as it is your right to travel, it is also his right to demand that your baby remain here. You have joint rights to her, and she is also his daughter. This is not China; this is a democracy. A while back I gave you a book on different forms of democratic government, so you can understand that you both have equal rights.

This was not the answer that I had wanted to hear. It is possible that if I had told her of Shaohan's outbursts, she might have changed her mind, but I was committed to leaving out that information from my story. I thanked her for the time she spent with me, and that she had agreed to listen to me and help me. She smiled and said, "If you need any more help, I am here at your service." Despite my disappointment, she left me with the feeling that she really meant what she said. I said goodbye and left the library quickly.

My quick steps woke up Ziyou who started to cry. With tears in my eyes, I looked for a quiet place to sit down and nurse her.

***

When I got home, I didn't even want to prepare my magic soup. I was confused and in an emotional state that didn't allow me to think of anything but my desire to take Ziyou with me to visit my parents.

Shaohan tried to speak with me gently in an effort to erase what had happened, but I still felt uncomfortable with him, or maybe it was convenient for me to use that to force him to agree to my trip. It was clear to me that he would never understand me, and as compensation for his dreadful behavior, I wanted him to at least agree to my plan.

I knew that I mustn't postpone the trip, that no time would be the right time; time was always a factor working against me, at least this was how I saw it until I arrived in Hong Kong. For years I tried to move time back to the evening before I was taken. I would imagine myself walking with Seyoung and convincing her to return home to eat more soup. I imagined this story so many times until I knew every detail, every stone on the way back home. Now I knew that time wouldn't return or stand still, and if I also submitted this time to its dictates, I would never travel to my parents.

The discussion with the librarian did not dissuade me from wanting to travel, though it definitely caused me to see what I was doing from Shaohan's point of view. I didn't tell her everything, and since I didn't reveal to her his violent behavior toward me, I had protected him and maybe myself, without realizing it, but her words about the baby echoed over and over in my head. I wanted to believe with all my heart that she was only expressing her opinion, but I couldn't disagree with what she had said. Shaohan was not just my husband, he was also Ziyou's father.

The thought of leaving my daughter behind was unbearable, and seemed impossible. There was no way that Shaohan could stop working, and even if he took time off, how would he handle her? The thought of my leaving her made me anxious. I didn't know if that was the result of my conversation with the librarian, or if it was my great love for Shaohan that had possibly been damaged.

Everything was swirling around together inside of me.

Sometimes it seemed to me that my trip was many years away; sometimes in my thoughts I ran away with my baby, and sometimes I traveled without her.

I pictured myself traveling both with Ziyou and without her. When I imagined the trip with her, I saw my parents hugging her, singing to her, being moved to tears. When I tried to imagine a visit without her, I couldn't think of anything. No music, no fragrance. I so wanted to pack a little bag and run away, and for that moment there was nothing I wanted more than to return to the country of my birth and my parents. I already knew where I would take the bus from to the border between Hong Kong and China in Shenzhen, and while I was still deep in my thoughts and planning, Shaohan returned from work. I didn't even notice that he had returned later than usual.

***

Shaohan sat on the chair and watched me nurse Ziyou. There was a pleasant quiet in our apartment. A family in a small room—a baby nursing and her parents sitting quietly, giving her the feeling of calm that she so needed. During those moments, there was no trace of the violent incident that had happened there, or the confused thoughts that were running around my head.

Shaohan waited for Ziyou to finish suckling, and began the longest speech that I had ever heard from him. He spoke without stopping, almost without breathing, as if he wanted to get across everything he had to say, and had planned to say it in one long sentence.

"I thought a lot about what happened and about what I did,

and also about what you did, and what you want to do." He swallowed hard and continued, "I have decided not to prevent you from traveling, though I believe it is a huge mistake, but I want Ziyou to stay here, and yesterday I already went to Lily the neighbor, and I spoke with her and her husband at length, and she is willing to have Ziyou stay with her, and we would pay her expenses, and salary for the care of the baby, and you have nothing to worry about, because if you don't want her to sleep only with me, I will visit her at Lily's every evening when I come back from work, and every morning when I wake up. I'll bring her diapers and everything necessary, and I very much hope that you will agree, because in this way you can travel and come back fast so that she will return home as quickly as possible, and that way we will all be together again…"

I listened to every word that he said and tried to understand how his proposal fit in with what I wanted. The thoughts swirled in my head with a terrible noise that prevented me from thinking, and required a major effort on my part to find a free space to organize my thoughts. I remembered the compromise that he had proposed way back when, so he could accept my reading books and visiting the library.

"How could I leave my baby with a strange woman?" I shouted, and hoped that this argument would convince him to let me travel with her.

"She is not a stranger," Shaohan answered quickly. "We know her and her husband very well, she is the one who helped you when it was hard for you in the first days after the birth, and I trust she will be able to help us now." Based on his articulate answer, I understood that he had prepared for this question in advance.

"It's hard for me to think of deserting my daughter," I said in desperation.

"You are not deserting her," Shaohan answered. "She is staying with me, I am her father. The neighbor is only helping us so you can travel in peace and return to us as quickly as possible."

"But it is important to me that my parents see their granddaughter," I tried a new direction.

"We'll go to the photography store and have them take pictures of her," Shaohan said with a smile, and I thought that he apparently had also prepared for this angle. "Who knows," he continued. "Maybe they'll give your parents a visa to visit us in Hong Kong." Now it was clear that Shaohan had arrived at this discussion prepared, and that I had no chance of convincing him. At least this time he expressed his wishes in words and not in a fierce tantrum, I thought, and that was enough to make me feel a bit better.

But still I was apprehensive and in another attempt to persuade him I said, "Shaohan, please think about it again. How will I be able to leave the baby alone and travel?"

"I am not preventing you from traveling," answered Shaohan in a steady voice, "but Ziyou is staying here, with me, and I hope you will return to us quickly."

I became angry again, and started to cry again. Shaohan did not get up and hug me, maybe so as not to raise expectations that he would change his mind. I sat next to Ziyou and sobbed. For years I had dreamed of returning home to my parents in the village—my yearning to see them had increased, but at that point it seemed that the chance to realize this dream was slipping away. The confusion caught in my throat, and I felt that I was suffocating. I started to cough and couldn't stop. Shaohan quickly brought me a glass of water and asked if he could help. I didn't answer him and continued to sob as

I watched Ziyou sleeping. I couldn't take my eyes off of her. I counted her little breaths, which were almost impossible to hear.

My throat burned and I tried to cough quietly. I had a hard time swallowing, and I felt burning in my lungs and abdomen. I didn't notice how much time I sat this way next to my baby daughter, watching her, staring into space and filled with self-pity. I considered giving up as I had when I was gripped by despair at the outpost in the rice fields, when I understood that I hadn't managed to escape. That was paralyzing despair. Now I was sitting on the floor, again paralyzed. I was about to desert my baby daughter, I thought to myself, and with each breath the thought shifted the pain across my entire body. I felt that I was shivering even though I wasn't cold.

There were moments when I decided to forget about the trip to the village of my birth, and there were moments when I looked at Ziyou and knew that she would manage without me for a few days. These thoughts were so agonizing, and when the night enveloped the apartment, I fell asleep with a painful body and a tortured soul.

***

Ziyou's gentle crying woke me, and my breasts were already dripping with milk. I saw Shaohan turn over in bed.

"I am nursing her and the neighbor has no milk," I burst out. "Their son was weaned long ago and she won't be able to nurse Ziyou." I knew that Shaohan didn't know how to solve that problem, but before he managed to say something I already answered myself, "Fine, I'll start to wean her and plan the trip. But before that, I want us to speak with the neighbor together; I must get to know her better and see how she gets along with Ziyou. Only then will I be able to travel without worrying."

The days following were terribly difficult. The pains in my chest were unbearable, and my rising temperature did not go well with my mental state. The neighbor bound my breasts with a cloth diaper, and commanded me not to remove it. Several times a day I placed cabbage leaves on my aching breasts according to her instructions, and when I removed them after several hours, they were wet, as if they had been soaked in a bowl of soup.

I asked the neighbor to stay with me for a few hours every morning so that I could see that she was indeed up to the task of caring for Ziyou while I was away. I already knew that I wouldn't travel for a long time. The trip itself would apparently take two or three days, and after a short visit at my parents' house, I would return immediately. For some reason, the risk of my being caught did not disturb me at all, maybe because I was completely involved with Ziyou and the neighbor who would be taking care of her.

I bought baby formula which was very expensive, and I also knew that the payment for her care would significantly reduce my savings, but at that time, finances were no object, in view of my strong desire to make the trip.

That same morning after Shaohan left for work, Lily the neighbor came. Though heavy, she was nimble. She boiled water in a pot to clean the bottles, prepared formula for the baby correctly, and asked me for permission to feed Ziyou.

Ziyou swallowed the liquid eagerly, and the neighbor found it necessary to apologize. "That's how it is with nursing babies," she said and smiled at me. "It is easier to eat from a bottle, and they eat much more and much faster.

I smiled back at her, and didn't know whether to feel relief or sadness. On the one hand, I wanted her to get along well with Ziyou, and on the other hand, it was painful to see my baby in her arms. Ziyou stopped eating, and Lily the neighbor put her on her shoulder and patted her back. The sound of the thunderous belch emerging from Ziyou's throat caused us both a good hearty laugh.

Lily laid Ziyou on her stomach on a small mattress on the floor, and went to wash the bottle. Ziyou wriggled restlessly, and I hurried to pick her up and was immediately hit by a shower of liquid spurting from her mouth. The sight of her spitting up and my wet clothes brought tears to my eyes, but Lily, who saw all this, was not fazed. She took Ziyou from me and told me to go get washed. She removed Ziyou's messy clothes and wiped her lightly with a damp cloth diaper. I stood frozen in awe of her calm manner.

"Go get cleaned up," she said to me calmly, as if no great drama had just taken place.

When I came out of the bathroom, Ziyou was already sleeping, her face quiet and her breathing relaxed. "The transition to formula is not easy for them," I heard Lily from behind me. I turned to her and listened. "They need to get used to the taste, and their digestive system has to get used to the new food," she added, "so you have no need to worry when she spits up in the coming days, nor if her diapers don't smell like, how shall we say, like flowers." We laughed again, and the tension that I felt slowly faded.

Lily's stay with me, which began with tension and suspicion on my part, became more pleasant, and I even wanted her to stay longer. "I'll come over again tomorrow," she said with a smile and left, leaving me in confusion and knowing that even if the process took some time, in the end I would leave Ziyou with her.

**

Until the day of my journey, every morning began with heaviness in my chest, which took me several long hours to release myself from. The struggle going on inside of me was tough, but I was still trying to overcome my fears and be able to wholeheartedly leave Ziyou in Hong Kong and make my trip.

Every morning Shaohan left for work and then Lily came up. Ziyou and I got used to her, and she got used to Ziyou. I didn't feel comfortable that I enjoyed her presence. I wondered if it was okay that I was fine with the fact that she was helping me, was with me at home, going out with me for walks with Ziyou, and even enjoying carrying her close to her body. I knew that I could count on her to take care of Ziyou.

The days passed, and I realized that I could set out on my journey. One morning I decided that I would travel a week from that day, thereby setting an exact date for the trip. I had already planned where and when to buy the bus ticket, and I knew that there was no turning back. In the meantime, I wanted to enjoy being with Lily a bit more; I knew that unfortunately after I came back she would no longer come to me every day to assist me and be with me.

In the evening, I told Shaohan that I was planning to travel the next week. His response was silence.

During that week Lily also taught me to prepare different kinds of foods, and every evening Shaohan gave me a grade for the dish we prepared that day. It was clear that our menu was going to change when I came back. I was happy for the connection created between Lily and myself, I felt that she did not arouse my curiosity like the smiling librarian, but I found in her a sympathetic ear and much practical advice that later helped me in raising my children.

The friendship with Lily reminded me of Seyoung, and only emphasized her absence. I promised myself that after the visit to my parents, I would find time to look for her. Many times I'd lie in bed and hug Shaohan from behind and imagine that it was Seyoung. I remembered how we slept in each other's arms on the shivery cold nights when we had no blanket. I remember how she had taken care of me after the punishment, how she washed the cuts left by the belt. To this day, any time I notice scars while showering, I feel heartache for Seyoung.

I told Lily my life's story, but I also spared her the hardest of the stories from the children's home, except for the description of the children who didn't wake up in the morning. Maybe the fact that I had a daughter to take care of made me think of this and increased my distaste for the ease with which the bodies of the children who had died were removed. Children who didn't eat enough, who froze to death because they had no way of getting warm, children who got sick and continued to go out every day for hard work in the fields until their little bodies surrendered.

Since I was in constant fear of someone reporting me to the authorities, I was extremely careful before the trip back to China. With Lily I spoke of my love of books, and about my language learning process, in reading books at the children's home, and she admitted that she didn't know how to read. The next day she came with a newspaper that her husband had brought home from work, and asked that I read her the head-lines. I was never very interested in newspapers, but reading the newspaper that Lily brought changed that.

Every morning when she came in with the newspaper, we waited for Ziyou to fall asleep and then we sat down to read with two cups of tea. After I finished reading Lily the head-lines, she chose an article that interested her and after we'd read the whole thing, we discussed it.

On the first morning we read together, I learned that a new shopping mall would be opening soon with stores selling all kinds of things from various countries. I was very curious about anything that taught me about other countries, and so I read the article with great interest. I learned the names of various fashion houses that had arrived from Europe, most of them from a country called Italy. I hadn't yet had the chance to read anything about that country, and made a note to ask the librarian some time. Products from famous sports brands, it was written in the article, would come from the U.S., and that giant country I was already familiar with. The word "brand" was new for me, and amused me for some odd reason.

I thought to myself how much I didn't know every time we finished reading an article in the newspaper. Fortunately, my curiosity helped me to overcome many gaps and be ex-posed to things in Hong Kong that I had missed in China. The next day, we read an article on page one on the new laws in Hong Kong, among them the restriction on air pollution on the island. In contrast with the imaginary world of books, the newspaper was full of information that sometimes was very interesting, but in most cases was only briefly presented and had no plot that developed. Slowly I understood the differ-ence between the newspaper articles and the books I loved so much. I distinguished between the different writing styles, and thought to myself that even though I was interested in the information that I received from Lily's newspapers, I still preferred reading books.

***

The article that Lily and I read discussed Chinese factories that emitted toxins, which were brought to Hong Kong via the clouds and wind. I had never given much thought to the subject of air pollution, and I certainly didn't know about any related problems. From the article, I learned that the factories in Hong Kong were held to restrictions to limit their emissions, but the Hong Kong government could not supervise what's done in China. The article brought statements by a senior minister who said that he planned to hold a global conference on the subject, to force China to solve the air pollution problem. As a result of the article, I decided to buy a cover for my mouth as soon as I could. I had already seen people walking in the streets with masks over their mouths, but in my innocence I'd thought that they were sick and didn't want to pass the illness on to others.

Two days before my trip, when the stomach pains and feelings of uneasiness that attacked me every morning had already worn me out, Lily came in without a newspaper and said, "Today I'm staying with Ziyou alone, and you can go by yourself to your library." My excitement at hearing this left me confused for a moment, and it took me time to realize that I was going out of the apartment by myself, without a baby carrier fitted around me.

I left the building to the unclean air of the city, but still breathed in deeply my new moments of freedom. I went to the bus station and noticed that my steps were light and quick, maybe because Ziyou wasn't on me, maybe because I was walking fast, or maybe because I felt, after a very long time, that I was allowed to do something that I liked without feeling guilty. I explained to myself that there was no choice but to finally leave Lily alone with Ziyou.

I arrived at the library out of breath, since I had run from the bus stop as if time would run out on me on the way. I found the smiling librarian sitting next to the check-out counter talking with one of the library patrons. I waved to her with both hands and went to choose a book from the shelf. I remembered that I wanted to read something related to that country named Italy, but I didn't find anything, or maybe I wasn't concentrating hard enough. I took a random book from the shelf, and sat down to read it, and then the librarian joined me, smiling as usual.

"You are positively glowing," she said and looked straight into my eyes.

"Did you notice that I am alone, without Ziyou?" I said with a smile.

"Now that you mention it, I did notice. So where did you leave her?" I saw signs of worry in her eyes, but I smiled broadly at her.

"She's at home with the neighbor, the one who's taking care of her when I travel in two days."

"Two days?!" she cried out.

"Yes, it's happening," I answered, and shivered. "I am traveling in two days to visit my parents, and Ziyou is staying with the neighbor." I was silent for a moment. Only after I had said these words aloud did I suddenly understand that it was really happening. In a minute I recovered and added, "And I hope to come back fast."

"I'm happy that everything is working out so that you can travel in peace," said the smiling librarian.

"You helped me a lot…" I said quietly. I felt the tears welling up in my eyes from emotion.

"I am happy to hear that," she answered and smiled her kind smile at me. Then she added, "I'll find you a few books so that you'll have something to do on the way.

The tension I felt in the morning was replaced with tears, but they weren't tears of anxiety but tears of gratitude that someone had thought of me, that someone cared about me. Besides Shaohan and Ms. Shuang, no one had ever wanted to bring me happiness, happiness that was all for me. The smiling librarian apparently felt awkward with the crying, because she got up and said quickly, "I'll come back a little later," and disappeared among the shelves. Somehow I managed to tell her that I wanted to read something about Italy.

I didn't manage to concentrate on the reading. My thoughts moved between my trip in two days and Ziyou's stay with Lily. In addition, I imagined the meeting with my parents exactly as I had imagined it all the years since I'd been taken away. I saw Lily hugging, feeding, and washing Ziyou, and all my apprehension from the fact that I had to leave my daughter with her disappeared. I still wasn't able to read, but I also didn't want to return home early and disappoint Lily who had given me the present of a few hours of reading.

I waited for the librarian to return with the books that she would suggest I take with me for the trip. I gazed at the shelves, but the words ran before my eyes, and I couldn't grasp their meaning. When the librarian returned with three books and a bright smile on her face, I tried very hard not to start crying.

"I brought you three translated books, as you like," she said happily. "I hope you enjoy them, and return them when you come back."

The librarian put the three books on the table. "The first is *Kaputt*[3] by Italian writer Curzio Malaparte, the second is by an author that I am not familiar with, but it discusses the fountains of Rome, and note you have been warned, I understand that whoever reads this book falls in love with the city of Rome. The last book is *Gone with the Wind*, an American classic written by Margaret Mitchell, and it's a book that everyone who loves books must read."

I got up from my seat, determined not to break the dam of water welled in my eyes, approached the librarian, and hugged her for the second time in my life. I felt her arms wrapped around me, and then the dam broke and the tears wet her shirt. We both started laughing. "Go on, get out of here," she said still laughing. "You are disturbing my work today." I actually was glad that she kicked me out of there.

I went out on the busy Hong Kong street with the three books, took a deep breath, and for the first time noticed that it was thick polluted air entering my lungs. People walked past me but didn't look at me. I was just another figure among the millions of people living with me during the same period of time, but not really in the same world. I knew that my trip to the village was the closing of a circle that would allow me to continue my life with a certain modicum of peace, and I hoped that I'd find answers to questions that I'd had for years.

---

3   Malaparte, Curzio. *Kaputt*. New York, E. P. Dutton & Co., Inc., 1946.

I returned home and surprised Lily who was playing on the floor with Ziyou, trying to make her laugh.

"So that's it?" she asked in amazement.

"Yes," I answered. "I took a few books to read on the trip. Besides that, I remembered that I'd wanted to take Ziyou to a photography shop, so that I could have pictures to show my parents." For a moment I looked down and was sad that I could take only a picture, and not Ziyou herself. After that I added, "That's why I returned early."

"Great idea," said Lily, pretending not to notice my sad eyes. "Let's get her dressed and I'll come with you to the photo shop."

When Lily got up from the floor, I hugged her as hard as I could. She was a little taken aback; maybe she wasn't used to getting hugs from people who were not family members, but I continued to hold her until I felt she was hugging me back. "I'll always remember that you made it possible for me to make a dream come true, and I'll always want only good things for you," I told her with great emotion.

***

We went out to the street with Ziyou in the baby carrier close to me. I had seen the photo shop many times on my way to the subway, but had never gone inside. Exactly when we wanted to enter the store, Ziyou started crying. I tried rocking her, but in the end we were forced to walk a bit down the street until she stopped crying and calmed down. When we returned to the store, we saw that there were people standing in line to be photographed and we had to wait. I stood and looked around me at the pictures of grownups and children hanging on the walls. Every one of them commemorated a moment in the life of the person in the photograph, a moment that he wanted to remember. I hoped that I would also remember this moment forever, the moment that my daughter was photographed. I hoped with all my heart that my parents would hang up the photograph of their granddaughter, and leave room for photos of other grandchildren.

The photograph was expensive for me, but I knew that a picture of Ziyou would be the nicest present that I could leave them when I left. I decided to be photographed with her. I sat on a chair across from the photographer and rested Ziyou on my lap, her head under my head, and her body stretched out on mine. The strong light of the camera flash surprised both of us. I was afraid that she would cry again, but she just blinked nonstop until we got home.

I put our picture on the dining table so that Shaohan could see it, and went to prepare supper for him. Lily left me with the words "We'll meet tomorrow, good night," and left me with Ziyou and the food preparation task. Shaohan arrived, and when he came to pick up Ziyou as always, he said as usual, "What a great smell! What did you two prepare today?"

When he sat down at the table, he saw our picture. "You went to the photographer?" he asked, surprised. And he suddenly looked crestfallen.

"I decided to photograph Ziyou so that I could leave my parents with a picture of their granddaughter. It was your idea," I said firmly. "Don't you remember?"

"Why didn't you wait so I could also be in the photograph with you?" he asked, insulted. "Are you ashamed of me? You don't want to show your parents a picture of me?"

I lost my breath and realized what I had done. The stress settled back into my rib cage like an iron ball bursting straight in. I didn't know what to say, and the only words that came out of my mouth were, "I'm sorry, Shaohan, I wasn't thinking…"

"You weren't thinking?" he yelled in anger. "You don't think of me anymore, yeah? Who else do you still think about besides yourself?" He got up from the chair and went into the bathroom.

I started crying, angry at myself for not thinking that it would be better for all of us to be photographed together. It was clear to me that I wasn't ashamed of Shaohan, and I would have been quite happy for him to come with me to my parents' house. I had been very excited to photograph Ziyou, and considered nothing else. Maybe I was angry that she was staying with him, and maybe for a minute I thought only of myself. I went into the bedroom, looked at Ziyou who was moving on the mattress just before falling asleep, lay down next to her and fell asleep completely drained.

***

My morning started a few minutes before Shaohan woke up, when I heard Ziyou moving and ran to pick her up, knowing that the next day I wouldn't be there, and would not be able to take her in my arms. My body trembled and I was in a cold sweat, my heart pounding quickly. I remembered that I'd had a frightening dream, but didn't manage to remember the details. Shaohan was still sleeping, and I thought to myself that he had gone to sleep angry. And I, who was supposed to leave on the most important trip of my life in a few hours, felt lost in my discomfort and mixed feelings, the frightening unsolved dream and the baby in my arms.

All the things that happened that morning, plus Shaohan's

shunning of me, caused me to walk around the apartment confused and unable to get organized. The whole time I couldn't remember what I had to do, and fortunately Lily came at some point to save me from the cold and awkward farewell from Shaohan. I tried to pack a bag to take with me, but I couldn't decide what to put in it. During the morning I showered three times and tried to put my thoughts together.

Finally, Lily came to my aid, and put into a little bag clothes and toiletries, and of course the three books that I didn't know I wouldn't read. She put the photograph into an envelope and carefully put it into the bag so it wouldn't get damaged.

But despite all her help, I remained confused the entire day and did not manage to decide what to do. Lily took care of Ziyou while I moved around the apartment without knowing what was going on with me. Even after Shaohan returned that evening, I didn't find the words, or his company.

At night I didn't close my eyes. I couldn't focus on any thought. The thoughts ran around my head like a movie running too quickly. I ran to the bus so as not to miss it, but didn't find the stop; I ran back and forth on the familiar street, but the bus stop had vanished. When I finally found the stop and boarded the bus, it drove somewhere else, changed direction, and traveled so fast, that I couldn't get off while it was driving. I sat on a bus traveling to a strange place that I didn't know, and I could only blame myself for what happened. I had made the choice to return myself to an unsafe place, a place that I would soon see how cruel it was, a place that I had no business going to, if only I had listened to my husband. I felt as if I was back on the truck taking me to the children's home, I again saw my mother running toward me. In the background I heard only the crying of children. I woke up in a cold sweat, and shook my head to chase the horror movie from my mind.

The next day I awoke at dawn, kissed Ziyou goodbye, and left for the bus stop with a bag in my hand and a great fear in my heart.

Home

I will never ever forget that ride. Not because it took two days, and not because it was bumpy and tiring, but because for the first time I was afraid of my fate.

I went to the bus station in Hong Kong by myself. Shaohan did not come with me, and did not say goodbye to me; he only said that he hoped they would let me return. This farewell hurt me greatly, and I thought about our relationship the whole way to the Shenzhen border. Only then did I know, I knew it because I felt it strongly in my entire body, I felt a hole open in my body that was big enough for my heart to fall out of. I knew that I loved him exactly the second that I boarded the bus, exactly when I took a step as part of my own choice, even though it was a step that angered him. I felt how important he was to me, that my life wasn't complete without him. Sharp pains pounded my temples. To the headache was added pain in the chest. This was the pain from words of farewell that were never said. We could have stood at the bus stop holding each other close, we could have kissed and kissed until the bus came, and he would have wiped away my tears. I would have gotten on the bus still feeling the place where he had hugged me tight in his arms. I regretted not telling him that I would return to him because I loved him with all my heart and soul.

Good-hearted Shaohan, who had picked me up off the street, taken care of me, who was a true friend to me, who had created new life with me alone in a strange place, I loved that man so much. But then I thought of his anger when he first heard that I wanted to return to my village, when I had read books, at my determination to make this visit. And I also couldn't understand how despite the fact that I had promised that this would be a visit that I would return from quickly, he still didn't give me his blessing for the journey.

From the many books that I had already read, I knew a lot about the complexity of relationships between couples, about those that had gotten through crises, and those that had broken up. I thought how in books it was always possible to find solutions for arguments, and it was possible to split lovers up, but in my life it was only me who was writing the story, so I had to write in precise words what I wanted and was willing to do, and what I could give up. I gave up a lot, but Shaohan didn't think so. I thought about how we had met and about our relationship, and asked myself if I would have fallen in love with him if he hadn't picked me up.

Shaohan had something hypnotic about him that caused all his friends to want to be near him, even those who worked with him at the hotel always sought to be near him and go out with him. I also loved his big heart and his true concern for those around him, but at the same time he had something aggressive that was evident not only on that terrible night, but also in the firm way he expressed his opinions, and in his inability to understand that another way was possible, that there were different people who thought differently from him, and liked things that he didn't necessarily like. When he encountered something that he didn't understand or didn't manage to connect with, he would respond in a disagreeable way. But I still knew that I loved him like I had never loved any man, partner, or friend.

I pondered for the first time my future after the visit. The baby would grow up a bit, I would return to working at the hotel, maybe I would go study. I wanted so much to be accepted for studies, to read, maybe I could become a teacher myself. Maybe I would study literature. Maybe I would even be a writer. My story was taking shape in the notebook, and I planned to finish the few pages remaining during my trip to China. I felt determined to study when I returned, determined as I had been to take the trip home in the first place. I could see myself studying every day. Studying, reading, and writing. Maybe I would write for a newspaper, the newspaper that the neighbor had brought me to read. Maybe I could earn a living from writing, how blissful that could be. These thoughts occupied me suddenly and caused me to smile.

The ride to the border continued for several hours and it seemed much longer than that. Possibly thanks to the fact that Shaohan had occupied my thoughts, I had been able to forget the fears that came with the return to China. Only when the bus stopped did I remember that exactly here, a little more than three years ago, my fate took an unexpected flip, and I received my freedom. My thoughts left Shaohan and returned to the waiting room at the border, and I saw the frightened little girl that I had been, whose ambitions to return to her mother were fading as time passed; I saw the teenager who learned to read and saw the world through books given to her by her teacher at the children's home.

And there I was again at the border crossing, but this time standing in line with people who were crossing the border in an orderly fashion; I did not look for breaks in the fence. I held a certificate testifying that I was a citizen of Hong Kong, which was supposed to allow me to return whenever I wanted to. But despite the fact that I had checked into this dozens of times at the Interior Ministry, everything regarding my rights and my status, when I approached the official who was supposed to stamp my passport, I was overcome with fear.

I felt beads of sweat on my face that ran down my body and into my pants. Every step I took made me a step closer to the front of the line, which intensified my pounding heart and hurt my chest. I was afraid that they would see the tension in my face and would want to investigate my past. I tried to slow my breathing down; I stopped the air in my lungs and released it slowly. I took another deep breath and tried to force air into my head. Just so I wouldn't faint and drop to the ground here, I thought. I stood behind a man in a blue suit and I knew that when he moved to the right, I would be meeting my fate. All my attempts to make time stand still failed, and suddenly I was facing the official behind the glass wall with the small window. "Papers!" he called out to me, and didn't even bother to look up. I put my passport on the little window sill, and lowered my head so that he couldn't see my face, which certainly gave away my anxiety. When I heard the two knocks of the stamp landing on the paper, I looked up at him. "Here," he said stretching out his hand to return the passport to me, and then impatiently asking that I not hold up the line for people standing behind me, and move aside. I hadn't noticed at all that I had frozen in place, and it was hard for me to believe that the whole thing had ended with two taps of the stamp. I pulled myself together and started to walk toward the door of the station. I had returned to China.

***

I didn't remember the view at the border at all, certainly not the skyscrapers that rose all around. I stopped awhile to take it all in, but then quickly ran to my connecting bus. I was curious to see how the border crossing the truck driver had left me at looked after the time that had passed. I looked for the excitement inside myself, but instead I only felt fear and curiosity when I stood again on Chinese soil. The place was no different from Hong Kong, certainly there was nothing to remind me of the children's home or the village. But I still sat down on a bench near the station and sought the excitement in returning to the land of my birth.

I have no idea how long I sat and stared into space, but I had no feeling at all that I had returned home. I walked to the stop for the bus that was supposed to bring me to the capital of the district, from which I would have to take another bus that would bring me to the village. I felt that I was at the beginning of the journey. I bought a ticket from the bus driver and sat next to the window expecting to see the views I remembered from my childhood, or the views that I wanted to remember.

The bus left to a flat landscape with no skyscrapers covering the sky, and though the tall buildings were replaced by shorter houses, nothing of what I saw was familiar to me. I tried to re-member the views of my childhood and strained to remember in particular the sight of the village. Would I recognize the vil-lage of my birth? Had there been many changes? My thoughts wandered from the sights outside the window to the inside of my parents' house. I remembered how the house looked; I still remembered the smell of incense that filled the room before we went to sleep. Despite my attempts to remember the houses of our neighbors and friends, I didn't manage to concentrate; the thought of my house was overpowering, and

I tried to picture the entrance to it. During all the years that passed I imagined how I would enter the house and find my mother and father sitting there waiting for me, but for the first time, different thoughts had taken control of my imagination.

Maybe I had a brother or sister? I thought. I even saw them sitting on the bed, waiting for my mother to finish making supper. My mother had given up on me and understood that they would not bring me back, I thought, and felt that the anger was starting to grow. When I entered the house, the thought continued, my cheeks already burning in fury, they would introduce my brother. What kind of parents would give up on their daughter that way and decide to have another child in her place? Now my entire body was filled with anger, and I even considered getting off the bus. During all those years I had been in pain from longing, I had never doubted my parents' attempts to bring me back, but just now on the way home I understood for the first time that maybe I had been abandoned, and it was possible that all the years of expectation and longing had been for nothing.

The landscape became more rural, mountains appeared from afar, and the sights were more familiar, but I still didn't want to reach the village. I didn't want to find out the truth about my parents. I already knew that I had been taken for re-education since that was part of the cruel policy of the regime in China. I also knew that they thought that I wasn't an only daughter since I was playing with the children of the night. But the fear that my parents, whom I had so much wanted to see again, had betrayed me, this fear broke my heart. Fate was being cruel to me again, I thought sadly, and if I had listened to Shaohan I would have stayed with him and held onto the possibility that my parents had been waiting for me. I could have gotten off the bus and returned to Hong Kong, but I had to find out the truth. I didn't want to live in doubt anymore, and so I was willing to face the truth and then after I had heard it, to hurt and to grieve, and then return to my new home and my little family – Shaohan and our daughter.

The longing for Shaohan and Ziyou mixed in my stomach with the anger and disappointment that I expected to feel when I entered the house, the home of my parents who had gone on with their lives, brought up other children, and provided them with a warm home, good food, warmth and love. What love is it possible to give to a child who comes instead of an abandoned child? There was really no logic in that. My parents had apparently turned into cold and dense people, I decided. The revolution led by the government had seized my parents too, and like many of the Chinese people, they also underwent brainwashing and became obedient people.

The bus continued on its route, the landscapes changed, the thoughts and anger increased, and every new picture that I saw from the window aroused my doubts regarding the visit home. Always when I had thought of the ride home, I had been excited by the very thought of it. Thousands of times I imagined the door opening and how I would be greeted. I imagined my mother running more quickly to me than she had run to the truck that had taken me from her. I wanted to hold on to my dreams, but for the first time since I had been taken, I couldn't help but think and understand that life in the village had continued after they had taken me and the rest of the children of the night. A new generation had been born to sleep at night, and my parents certainly had had another child who could play during the day.

Signs

The bus stopped. Though the landscape was familiar, I had never seen a paved road in the village. I got off the bus slowly, my pack on my back. I stood for several long minutes with my back to the bus, even after it had driven away. I don't know if I was afraid or maybe excited, but my body surrendered to an uncontrollable internal voice and I froze in place.

I moved my head slowly to see where I was and what I remembered of the village of my birth. The landscape above the roofs of the houses was familiar, but these houses hadn't been there during my childhood. I didn't recognize the location of the bus stop, and I didn't manage to figure out where my house was or where it had been. My legs trembled and I couldn't move them. I stood there for a long time, and slowly the sights returned to me, as if I had been there just yesterday. I saw my mother lying on the ground screaming at the police officer, and I was afraid that I too would fall. I begged my legs to carry my body until I got used to the idea that I was finally there, until I managed to walk.

An old man walked by and asked if I needed help, and I couldn't even answer him. I looked at him for a long time and hoped that I would recognize him or he would recognize me, but he continued on his way until I could no longer see him.

My bag was very heavy and I looked around for a rock or a bench that I could sit down on before continuing. When I turned my head to the left I saw a stone wall around one of the houses, and decided to try to walk over to it and lean on it.

My legs were heavy, and each step I made toward the house seemed to require a supreme effort, and my body didn't seem to be working in coordination with my wishes. I didn't know whether the thoughts that had occupied me the entire way had worn me out, if the fear of crossing the border had weighed on me, or if it was the dread of what I would find at my parents' house that was making my body struggle with my wishes. It occurred to me that years of longing to return to the village were liable to end in my death on a paved road without shoulders. This thought seemed to prod me on, and after a while I reached the stone wall and leaned on it. At first the coolness of the stone wall, which took some of the weight off me, was pleasant to me, but at some point I felt pain in my back from the sharp stones protruding from the wall. I then sat on the cold concrete ground and relaxed all the muscles in my body, and for a moment I truly rested. In the familiar landscape that surrounded the village I managed to recognize some houses among the newer two-story buildings. I tried to remember how the village had been based and focused on the houses that I did recognize. I knew that if Shaohan had been there with me, I would already have been sitting in my parents' house drinking tea.

After the tough argument with Shaohan about the trip, I had thought that my anger would cause me not to miss him, but instead I found myself thinking about him and Ziyou no less than about the people I would meet in the village.

The thoughts pushed away the pain that the protruding

stones had caused to my back, but replaced it with a deeper pain. I had the feeling that I had been sitting on the sidewalk for several hours. Many people had passed by me, but I didn't recognize any of them, and they didn't say anything to me; they just looked at me with curiosity and moved on quickly. My clothes apparently gave me away as a foreigner, and so they apparently chose not to have anything to do with me. It was clear to me that I would never move from the place where I was resting if no one helped me, and so I weakly asked a woman passing by with a large basket, "Excuse me! Excuse me, miss, could you help me?"

Though I had yelled, no sound emerged, and only after I repeated the yell a few times did I manage to get a sound from my throat, and the woman approached me. I tried to look at her from close up, maybe I would recognize her, but I couldn't see her face clearly in my exhaustion and desperation. "What do you want, miss?" she asked, and bent down to hear me better. I took a deep breath so that I could speak to her clearly, and she stood there and waited patiently. I felt her hand move the hair from my face, she apparently was trying to figure out who I was.

I couldn't speak, and her touch filled my eyes with tears. I put my head down, and the only thing I felt was the woman's hand patting my head. I didn't hear what she said, but her voice was pleasant and I didn't want her to stop caressing me. Even when the tears had dried, I couldn't pick up my head and explain to her what I was doing there. From the big basket she had put on the ground, she took out a rolled-up banana leaf. Her caressing hand took my trembling hand; she put the leaf in it and opened it so that I could eat the sticky rice. Since I had escaped from the children's home, I had refused to eat rice from a leaf. Any time I saw a rolled-up banana leaf filled with rice at the many stalls in Hong Kong, and at temples I entered, I would feel sick, as if I was about to vomit.

After a while, the caresses stopped and I heard the steps of the woman moving away from me. I still hadn't moved from the wall and hadn't picked up my head, but when I started to feel cool air through my clothes, I looked up and saw that evening had fallen. A few lights were on in the houses, and now I no longer recognized the village that I had remembered for so many years. If I stayed like that, I thought to myself, I would freeze to death and they would find me lying there like they had found Anchi in the children's home. I remembered that her body had been completely blue before she was wrapped in a white sheet. I pushed away the terrible thought and looked at my hand. I saw that the leaf with the rice was still sitting on it, and I decided to overcome the disgust and eat a bit of the rice in the hope that I would have the strength to get up.

The cold sticky rice stayed in my mouth, and I didn't manage to swallow it. When I couldn't deal with the terrible taste in my mouth, I managed to get up onto my knees, spit out the rice, and vomited what little was in my stomach onto the sidewalk next to me. I couldn't bear the smell of the vomit, and the fact that I was already on my knees helped me get up and stand on my feet. My weak body moved slowly, but with the last of my strength I lifted the pack onto my back and decided to go from there and start looking for my parents' house. I walked slowly along the street, trying to identify the houses along the way. It was clear that the village had grown. Darkness took over every corner, and I hoped I would be able to hear the children of the night playing.

***

I took a deep breath of the familiar night air, and my steps became lighter. I walked in no particular direction and looked for signs of the village that I had left. I looked for my parents' house that I had known so well and remembered every detail of. I passed several houses that looked familiar to me, but I couldn't remember who lived in them. A few boys were walking behind me who apparently had just returned from working in the fields. I decided to ask them for help, but before they got to me, they turned and entered one of the houses. I continued walking, searching for familiar sights. I approached houses that had lights on and looked for hints to my past, clues that would lead me to my mother and father.

When I felt that desperation was crawling and climbing along my body, I turned right onto one of the narrow streets, and there was Dewei-Hu's house. He was not just a neighbor but a good friend. I remembered the wagon that he had built for my mother so that she could walk around the village with me and the three Changs. I started to move quickly toward his house, the whole time feeling nothing but my own breathing, which became stronger in my head. Finally, I was standing by the door. I looked around me for my parent's house, but there was no building that looked like what I remembered as my house. I remembered that from our house you could see Dewei-Hu's. I remembered myself standing on our threshold and waving to him when he came out of his house. From his house, I should have seen my parents' house, but I did not see anything similar to it at all.

Dewei-Hu's house was set between two two-story stone houses, which apparently had been built recently. Before I went further, I tried again and again to find my house, look-ing in every direction, listening carefully, and trying to sense a familiar smell. My hand touched the door handle, but I stopped myself and didn't push it to enter. Maybe someone else was living in his house. I realized that I must not burst in like that! I pulled my hand back and knocked lightly on the door. When no one answered, I waited a few minutes, took a deep breath, and waited a bit more before possibly revealing my fate. I knocked again.

"Come in!" I heard a voice, and entered. Dewei-Hu was sitting at a small dining table, his head bent over. His hair was gray and his face all wrinkled, but his eyes were lively. I hadn't remembered him like that, but I recognized him immediately. I remembered that he was short and much older than my father, but he had always been active and sturdy. He looked up at me, and when he saw me he greeted me with the same smile I knew so well.

I moved toward him and looked around, looking for clues. I didn't remember his house. There was no smell of cooking, nor the fragrance of incense that I had remembered, the incense that the people in the village would light before going to sleep. I approached him as he was getting up slowly from the chair, I fell into his arms and cried into his chest. Dewei-Hu hugged me softly. I was taller and wider than he was, but he slowly tightened his grip, until it was impossible to detach my body from his body.

Finally, I picked up my head and looked over his shoulder. "Where are my parents?" I asked. Dewei-Hu continued to hug me tightly until it was hard for me to breathe, and he didn't let go. I moved uncomfortably, trying to take stolen breaths between the sobs. He didn't answer my questions or say anything at all. After a while, he loosened his grip and sat heavily on the chair. He looked at me, his eyes brimming with tears, and suddenly covered his face with his rough hands. I had never seen him cry, and he wanted to hide it from me, but his sobbing could be heard from between his hands.

"Where are my mother and father?" this time yelling at him, not letting feelings of compassion distract me. He motioned with his hand for me to sit opposite him, and I quickly sat down and waited for him to speak.

"Since the night that you were taken away, your mother and father never stopped looking for you," he started to say, all choked up, attempting to overcome his tears. "At first they traveled to all kinds of places to look for you. Anyone who knew anything and told them about places where children who had been taken from their homes were being held, gave them hope that maybe you were there, and they hurried to travel and look for you at those places. After searching for you at several of these places, they went to the court in Beijing with your birth certificate. The process was very long, and they traveled often to the big city to find out if there was any more information or if it had been decided to release you yet. Your father had stopped working in the fields, and your mother had stopped working in the packaging house and devoted all her days to finding you. They were helped by neighbors who knew how to read and write, and I also tried to help them with my contacts with neighbors in other villages, to find out where you had been sent. They sent hundreds of letters to anyone they thought might know something. That was all they did, and for a long time, I too was completely involved in that."

He was quiet for a moment, took a deep breath, and continued, "After several years they received a letter that authorized them to pick you up at the children's home where you were. The very next day they rode there together, but when they arrived, they found out that you had run away a month before. When your parents tried to understand where you had run away to, the principal of the children's home refused to cooperate. She screamed at them that she was angry at what you had done, and soon kicked them out of the place, without their understanding from her where you had run to or where you were."

Dewei-Hu kept hiding his face in his hands and crying. My eyes brimming with tears, I waited a moment until he lifted his head again. He continued, choked up, "Your mother did not talk much when she returned to the village, and she lay in bed all day and cried. She refused to eat or drink, and stopped lighting incense. All attempts by your father to encourage her to continue looking for you failed. The neighbors tried to get her out of the house, but even if she did agree to get up and go out a bit, she soon returned to bed."

Dewei-Hu sighed, and continued more quietly, "Three months later she died. The doctor told your father it was from a broken heart…" There was silence, and I got on one knee and hugged him. This time, his body was limp in my arms. He sat petrified on the chair and refused to lift his head. "Dewei-Hu," I said quietly, "Where is my father? I don't see the house…" Dewei-Hu wiped his lips which were wet with tears, straightened up a bit and said faintly, "Your father died a few months ago; I didn't ask from what because it was clear that without his wife he wouldn't last very long."

My heart pounded. I was too late. The pain of sorrow spread within me, and all I could do was cling to the knowledge that they had looked for me, they had tried to bring me back, that they wanted me and loved me. This knowledge did not comfort me very much. I waited for the crying and pain to fill me, but before I fell completely into the abyss of loss, I wanted to tell Dewei-Hu that I had a daughter.

"I want to tell you something joyful," I finally said, in a voice that was somber but clear. I looked at his thin, gray hair and remembered how my mother would cut his hair when he would come to eat with us, and I would watch her in admiration. Dewei-Hu still hadn't lifted his head, but his crying had stopped and I saw that he was listening to me. "My parents have a granddaughter. Her name is Ziyou, and right now she is with her father in Hong Kong."

Dewei-Hu looked at me with teary eyes. He wiped them with his sleeve, and in a voice trembling with emotion he asked, "Does she sleep at night?"

9 781729 362891